Noah Tone

Plague of Powers

Noah Cotter

First Edition

PAGE PUBLISHING, INC.
Conneaut Lake, PA

First originally published by Page Publishing 2020

ISBN 978-1-64628-448-1 (pbk)
ISBN 978-1-64628-450-4 (hc)
ISBN 978-1-64628-449-8 (digital)

Printed in the United States of America

For my Grandpa Rick, hope you are proud of me.

Part One

CHAPTER 1

Bad Medicine
Dr. Parkins

Dr. Parkins's eyes widened in amazement as he read the readings. It was truly unreal. He had found the cure to cancer. He quickly walked over to his desk, where the cure lay still in the vial to the right of him. He was furiously jotting down notes when suddenly his patient, Emma, started to make a gurgling noise.

"Emma?" he asked.

She was now clawing at her throat.

"Emma!" he said louder this time. He raced to the side of her bed. She was straining to breathe. He swung his head around to look at the readings. They were off the chart! But it wasn't the cancer that was going haywire. It was something else.

"Aaargh!" Emma screamed. Her neck was bulging, and her eyes looked like they would pop out of their sockets.

"Emma! Answer me!" he yelled. *Snap!* Then one of the braces on her bed snapped. *Snap! Snap!* He backed away in horror. No one in all his years of fighting cancer had done such a feat. *Snap!* The last brace came undone, and without warning, a gust of wind knocked him off his feet. Dazed, he looked up and saw Emma floating in mid-air with papers, pencils, and other medical supplies zooming around and around her in a vortex of wind. It was the most amazing and most horrifying thing he had ever seen.

The wind intensified, and he had to hold on to the side of the bed or else he would be sucked into the storm.

Emma stared at him, her eyes glowing an eerie silver, and she focused all the wind into his stomach. *Thump!* He felt his rib crack, and he flew into the cold brick wall.

Crack! He heard the sound of breaking bones, and a burning pain shot up his left arm.

"Ooooh…" He groaned, then his instincts took over. His eyes darted to where the cure had been laying on his desk. It was gone.

"No!" he yelled. He tried to get up, but the wind flew under him, and he shot upward.

For a split second, he saw someone standing in the doorway. Then everything went black.

Chapter 2

Story Time
Noah Tone

I never meant to make anyone mad, let alone make someone want to kill me, but fate has its ways, I guess.

To start off, my name is Noah, Noah Tone. And I'm about to tell you a pretty crazy story, from my perspective, at least. It doesn't matter if you believe this story or not. The choice is totally up to you. I won't be insulted if you don't believe this story. I will definitely understand. At first, I didn't believe it as well, but now it's the most real thing I've ever known.

But before story time starts, you've got to get to know me, the main character of this story. I am short, period. But I make up for that in plenty of ways. I am part of the wrestling team at my school and the basketball team, and I have a lot of friends. It may seem like I'm well-off, but it seemed to only make me more of a target in the first place. I also have something unique and different about me. It's not a disorder, down syndrome, autism, or cancer. It's something special, but I think you'll catch on early in the story.

Now to start.

CHAPTER 3

Dressed and Ready Noah Tone

"Noah, it's time to get to school!" Was it Mom or Dad this time? "Noah, come down and eat your breakfast! I spent a hard deal of work on it for you!" Mom, definitely Mom.

"Mom! Just a few more minutes!" I begged.

"Boy, that's an interesting thing to hear from a fifteen-year-old whose wrestling final is today!" my mom shot back.

"Whoa! I forgot!" I shot out of bed, ignoring the messed up and wrinkled sheets of my mattress. I quickly packed my wrestling jersey and equipment into my backpack. I raced to the side of the railing just outside of my room in the hallway.

"Mom, I'm ready!" I shouted over the railing. She looked up at me, and her expression turned incredulous.

"Where exactly do you think you're going?" she asked, still stunned.

I looked at myself. I was still in my underwear.

My sister, Anna, stepped next to my mom.

"I've heard excitement can make people do some crazy things, but this is the worst I've seen in person," she remarked.

"Very funny," I shot back. As I was walking to my room, I rolled my eyes. My mom told me that having a twelve-year-old sister is a blessing, but sometimes I think otherwise. The deal that she has x-ray vision furthermore weighs to the fact.

I quickly dressed myself, not caring about how messy my hair looked. I couldn't be late to the final. My team was counting on me. I raced down the stairs, practically waiting for my dad to say something.

"Noah! You're gonna break those railings!" he said a little too fast.

"They're fine, Dad, I'm pretty sure that you spent too much time fixing them last year. But at least it's paid off," I reassured him.

My dad restored old houses and sold them. In other words, you could call him a house flipper. My mom stayed at home and took care of the kids, at least the one who didn't go to school yet.

"So I heard Mom took her time on the breakfast. What is it?" I asked.

Seth, my ten-year-old brother, sniffed the air. "Bacon…eggs… and cinnamon rolls," he said slowly.

"Mmmm…," I said.

"How do you know?" Dad asked. "She hasn't even brought out the food yet."

Seth looked down at his feet.

"You used your gift, didn't you?" he said sternly.

"Yes, sir, I did," he said innocently.

"You know the rule, your gift is yours to keep, not to share!" my dad put out. "The sooner you guys figure that out, the better!" he said.

"But—" Jesi started.

"Don't but me! You may not be old enough to be punished, but you should have a good idea of what's going on!" my dad shouted.

Jesi, my six-year-old brother, loved using his gift. He probably was the worst with keeping it a secret.

"I wouldn't consider it a gift. I like to think of our gifts as superpowers," my sister said casually as she trotted to her seat. My dad raised his eyebrows. "A superpower that is best not to use on the world," she added. "You should think of yourself like made-up superheroes like Batman or Superman. They tried to keep their powers a secret."

"Well put, Anna," my dad complimented.

"I like to think of you as squirrel girl," Seth smirked. Jesi laughed out loud.

"At least I don't listen to every sound someone makes when they go to the bathroom!" Anna shouted back.

"That was only for fun! And at least I can't *see* the things someone does when they go to the bathroom!" he shot back.

They were both in each other's faces now. "Come on, guys, no need to set a scene," I put in. "It was entertaining though!" Jesi giggled.

I looked at my watch, 8:30 a.m. I needed to get to the finals and quick. The matches started at 9:00 a.m. It was a good thing we lived close to the high school.

Mom handed me my plate. "Eat up! It's almost time to go!" she said enthusiastically.

"And don't you dare use your power out there. That's the worst form of cheating that you could possibly do," my dad said sternly. "I never once had a gift like you, but I would never use it to my advantage."

Ha. Easy for him to say. I still remembered the last time I used my powers at a basketball game, when I'd forced the basketball a little to the left a bit so I would make the three. Even though I was praised for making the game-winning shot, my dad had locked me in my room for two days. I still won't forget that. But me and my siblings always got away with using our powers when my parents weren't looking. It kind of turned into a habit after a while.

I looked at Levi, my thirteen-year-old brother, and the only person who hadn't spoken so far at the breakfast table, or in his life for all that I knew. I didn't know much about his gift, other than the fact that my parents had told me that he can see stuff before it would happen, whatever that means.

I'd just finished my last bit of egg when my dad stood. "Time to go, bud. Let's win this thing!" he said.

"You can count on it," I replied. And just after me and my dad stepped out the door, I forced it to shut behind me using my gift. What were they so afraid of?

Chapter 4

Wrestling with Sound
Noah Tone

While I was driving in the van with my dad, I thought about my question. What were they so afraid of? The only way to figure out was to ask my parents themselves, but something in my gut told me not to. It wasn't that my parents were abusive or cruel. They'd been good to me my whole life. It was just that I felt like the answer was something that I wouldn't want to hear.

"Dad?" I asked.

"Yes?" he replied.

"I've been wanting to ask you a question for a long time, but I was afraid that you wouldn't like to hear it, and that I wouldn't want to hear the answer," I said slowly.

My dad straightened up in his seat so he could see me in the rearview mirror. "You can tell me anything you want to, Noah," he said in a tone that I didn't recognize.

"Well, it's just that it seems like you and Mom have been a little, you know, overprotective about our gifts for as long as I've known," I said heavily. It felt like a weight had been lifted off my shoulders.

"Are you questioning my authority?" he said coolly.

I tensed up in my seat. "No, I was just wondering if there is a reason why you don't want us to use our powers," I pushed.

My dad sighed. "Noah, sometimes knowledge can be a burden. Are you sure you want to know?"

Suddenly I realized that he and my mom were doing this for a reason. I couldn't control my curiosity. "Yes, sir," I said smoothly.

"Well, you are getting older. It would only make sense that you know the truth," he said heavily. I felt like he had felt just as good as I did to get problems off his shoulders.

Bzzz! Bzzz! His phone was ringing. I wanted to use my gift so bad to stop the ringing, but I knew better. "Sorry, gotta take this call," he said happily. It seemed as if he was happy not to tell me the truth.

I huffed in frustration. "So close," I mumbled under my breath. "So close."

Once we opened the high school doors, noise flooded our ears. I used my gift to drown out the sound. I liked things orderly and quiet. My gift was the one in the family that I could get away with the most.

We stepped into the gym, my dad still holding the phone to his ear. "Go meet up with your team, bud. The matches are about to start," he said to me.

I watched him take his place in the bleachers, and I went into the bathroom to change. Once I stepped out, I was met by two large figures, Sam and Isaac.

Sam and Isaac were the worst bullies in school. I wouldn't be surprised if they were the worst in the world. They'd beaten some people so badly that some had to go to the emergency room. At least I'd been told.

"Hey, look. It's Mr. Hotshot of the wrestling team." Sam smirked.

"Come on, gimme what you got, mousy wousy!" Isaac taunted.

I knew better than to mess with them. Everyone knew better. "Look, guys. I don't want any trouble. I really need to get to my wrestling team," I explained.

"Oh, but you've made yourself trouble!" Isaac spat. "You told Dr. Foston about that person we beat up last week. We had detention for a whole week because of you!" he yelled.

"You guys should be used to getting in trouble, and that person you beat up was Dr. Watson's son, Zane," I shot back.

"I'm warning you. Just give us what money you've got, and we'll let you go." Sam sneered.

"You guys deserve to have detention the rest of your whole miserable lives, and to tell the truth, it was Drew Bower who told the principal!" I said confidently. Big mistake.

"Why you—" Sam growled.

"Now you're gonna get it!" Isaac roared.

I tried to run around them, but Isaac grabbed me by the arm and slammed me into the wall. My ears started to ring. I quickly drowned the ringing out with my gift.

"We warned you..." Issac sneered, close enough I could smell his breath. Moldy cheese and onions. I nearly gagged. If Seth smelled this, he would pass out probably.

I fought against his grip, but he was too big, and I was too small.

"I got him pinned, Sammy. Give him everything you've got."

Sam slowly walked up to me. "No one smart enough has ever talked to us like that." He smiled wickedly. "Any last words?"

I was sweating but shivering at the same time by now.

"Ha! I bet little mousy's wet himself already!" He laughed.

Okay, this had gone too far. Now my fear was replaced by anger. I could blast these creeps out of the universe if I wanted to.

"Actually, Sam, I do have some last words," I said smiling.

Sam frowned. "Okay, but make them quick. I don't have patience when it comes to beating up people," he spat at me.

"Oh, trust me, I'm sure you can wait a little longer," I said.

"Hurry up," he growled.

"Don't expect me to come to your funeral," I said slowly.

"Huh?"

Vrrrrrrrrrrr! The room erupted in sound waves. Isaac flew headfirst into a toilet, and Sam's face hit the mirror with so much force the glass cracked. Toilets came undone, and a sink hit Isaac in the butt.

Vrrrrrr... I let the sound waves die down.

I walked over to Isaac and took him out of the toilet by his pants. I placed him down next to the toilet roll, then I got Sam and set him next to Isaac. Isaac was coughing out blood and toilet water. He started at me as if I was the devil. Sam was knocked out, his nose crooked.

I got in Isaac's face. "That enough to wet your pants? Don't you dare pick on me or my friends, or next time I'll dunk you further into the toilet!" I yelled in his face. "And if you tell anyone about this, I'll personally shoot you to the Grand Canyon. And if you're smart, you'll know that's about five states away from here. Tell Sam the same." When I was about out of the stall, I said, "And get some mouthwash!"

As I was walking out, I heard the faint sound of Isaac crying. In spite of breaking Dad's rules, I smiled to myself.

I ran straight to my team. There was no time to spare. I was only in the huddle for about thirty seconds when the horn blew. It was time to wrestle.

The matches were great, with Devin Wassmen winning with a single-leg takedown and Jake winning with a chest-lock turn.

The coach, Mr. Middleston, leaned down and whispered in my ear, "Why were you so late today? It's the final, you know."

"I was stopped by some kids in the bathroom," I said casually.

"Did they do anything to you?" he asked.

"They didn't get the chance to," I said happily.

Mr. Middleston chuckled and patted me on the back. "Looks like those wrestling moves have paid off!" he said.

I grinned up at him. Mr. Middleston was the most understanding guy I've ever met.

I looked up at my dad. He looked down at me then nodded toward the mat. I looked over. It was my turn next. I would make my team and my dad proud.

My name was called, and I stepped onto the mat, me and my opponent crouching in our positions. This guy kept getting closer and closer to me, forcing me to move back. His stance was perfect and unchanging. I could tell right off that this wouldn't be an easy match.

Suddenly, he pounced me, forcing me on my heels. I fought back, but that's what he wanted. He easily slid down to my legs, grabbing them in a double-leg takedown. I crashed onto my back. Everything seemed to go into slow motion. I remembered the score. It was tied. This was the last match. The moment he pounced, I rolled to the side. He hit the mat with a thud. Grasping for me, but getting nothing but air. I rolled over on top of him. He was down. First round, my win.

The rounds went through hard and unchanging. Tie, tie, tie. It was my last chance, the last round, the score tied 14–14. I couldn't fail. I was the best member on my team, and I couldn't let them down.

We circled, both of us tired and weary. And to my surprise, he pounced me at the exact moment he did the first round. I should've known what was coming. But I was struggling against him again on my heels. He slid down for my legs and went for the double-leg takedown, again. I fell on my back, landing with a dull thump. I saw him for a split second in the air, almost on top of me. I was going to lose. There was no time to roll to the side this time. And without thinking, I surged. He flew back all of a sudden, landing three feet away from me. It must've looked unreal to the crowd. They all oohed. I jumped on top of him, quicker than lighting, and ending the match.

The gym erupted in noise and whistling. Then the sound drowned out without me even using my powers. I looked into the bleachers at my dad. He had seen it. He was eyeing me with a stare that would send you reeling. A wave of terror washed over me. What had I done?

Chapter 5

Taken
Noah Tone

My team rushed me, jumping on top of me, slapping my back, and screaming. I quickly pushed away from them, feeling nothing but guilt.

"You did awesome, dude!" Easton yelled over the noise.

"You can say that again!" Hampton screamed. "We won it! We really did!"

I was met by countless more compliments and congratulations. But I pushed past every one. I didn't plan to stay for the medal ceremony. My dad would be even angrier if he saw me with a medal I didn't deserve. I was about to walk through the doors when a girl stopped me. It was Ava, one of the popular girls. As much as I desired to talk to her, now was not the time. I tried to get around her, but she stopped me again.

"Look, I didn't do anything to you, and I can't talk to you right now."

"That's not right, Noah. You just won the whole tournament, and you're gonna leave?" she asked.

"Look, it's none of your business, so just leave me alone," I said angrily.

As I was walking out the door, she said, "You didn't really win the match, did you?"

I stopped in my tracks then slowly turned my head toward her. "You watched the match." Great, that would make her think she's right about me not really winning it.

"Every bit," she said sternly.

"You're the last person I would talk to about this," I said.

"You can trust me. I have something special like you too. I just need to know what you can do, then I'll tell you about me."

Was she luring me into a trap? Was this the danger that my dad was talking about? Now if I was a father, I'd do the same he did to us. I knew my dad would kill me if I told her, but if she had a gift too, that would make me feel a lot less than a freak.

"Okay, but we need to go someplace where people won't hear us."

"I know a place!" she said a little too loud. "Follow me!"

She was literally running, and I had to jog so I wouldn't lose her. We went all the way to the back of the school when she stopped.

"This should be far enough," she gasped.

"Ya think?" I said.

"You can never be too careful," she panted. "Now, do you feel safe to tell me about what you did back there?" she asked fast.

"Wait a minute, I need to know that your special thing about you isn't like a disorder or something, 'cause then this would just be a waste of time," I fired back.

She put her hands on her hips. "Do you really think I have a disorder?"

I smiled. "Okay, so you may look pretty, but I'm not taking any chances."

"No, for your information, what I have is rarer than any disorder," she said.

"Okay, I'll tell you, but you have to promise not to tell anyone," I said seriously.

"Cross my heart," she replied.

"I know it may sound crazy, but I can manipulate sound."

"So you're like a radio or something, 'cause that doesn't explain how you flipped Chuck Norris off you," she said, irritated.

"I'm not finished. I can create sound waves that are powerful enough to probably destroy this building, although I don't know actually how powerful the waves can get," I said expectantly.

"That's really cool, but how did we not hear anything when you used sound waves to get Norris off you?" she questioned.

"I can control how loud and soft things get," I explained.

"That's totally awesome!" She beamed.

"Sometimes it's not as great as you may think," I said, looking at the ground.

"I understand. Being different isn't easy," she said sadly.

I changed the subject. "So you said you have some power too?" I asked, waiting for something small and useless, like most of my brothers' and sister's gifts.

"I can control gravitational pull," she said, waiting for me to say something like, "Whoa! That's, like, a superhero power!" Which it was, but it took me a while to process it.

My mouth was literally hanging open when I said, "You can what?"

She giggled. "Yep, that's what I said."

"So you can, like, make me float?" I asked.

"Yes! But there's also something else that's not too fun I can do. I can increase the gravitational pull," she said, looking scared.

"What's so bad about that?" I asked.

"No, it's like squish you down like a pancake pull," she said slowly.

"Oh, well, don't use me as your testing dummy!" I said, acting scared.

She laughed.

"I've got to go, but I'm sure we'll talk soon," I said.

"That's fine. I've got to go too," she replied. "Catch you later!" She flipped her hair around and walked away. I needed to go too, even though I didn't want to meet my father at the moment.

I went into the bathroom, with Isaac still there. When he saw me, he said, "Please don't hurt me," weakly.

"I want to, but I don't feel like it," I said in a sad tone. I went into the stall next to him and got dressed. Then I bolted out of the bathroom. The longer my parents waited for me, the angrier they would get.

As I opened the door, I felt a drop of rain hit my face. I needed to get into the van. But usually my whole family came to pick me and my dad up in the van right by the curb, but the van wasn't there. They probably parked somewhere after waiting for me. Dad probably already told Mom about what happened. She probably wasn't mad. She probably felt sorry for me. What would happen to me? Would my dad lock me in my room for three days now? The thought sent chills down my spine even though the rain was cold.

I stepped onto the street, the pavement squeaking under my new sneakers. I didn't take a step when a cold hand covered my mouth.

I tried to scream, but I couldn't speak. I had to use my gift. This was serious. I turned the volume in the man's ears up enough to make him deaf, and he immediately dropped to the ground, screaming. Suddenly, I saw a club swing toward my head. I was too slow. *Thunk!* I fell to the ground, grimacing in pain. A hand grabbed my jacket, picking me up easily. I looked into his eyes. This was no joke. He was dressed in a black suit and had black boots with metal tips. He must've been around seven feet tall and strong enough to be in world wrestling.

"Don't think about using any tricks, or we'll use some tricks of our own," he growled. Out of the corner of my eye, I saw the man I had nearly turned deaf stand up.

"I say we throw him down a storm drain. He's a rebellious one!"

I whimpered. "Take it easy on the kid, Sipes. They're all scared at first."

I sighed in relief. At least this guy was reasonable. *But what did he mean by 'They're all scared at first'? Had they been kidnapping people for a living?*

Suddenly the man laughed. "I'm sure that the boss will do something much worse to him if he does anything like that at training!"

Training? I mustered all my strength not to scream for help.

"Whatever," Sipes said. "Throw him in the car."

The other man strapped me down to a seat. I looked over. It was Levi! He had been kidnapped too? I couldn't look behind, but I didn't need too.

"They took everyone. They took the whole family," Levi whispered.

I was amazed. It was the first time I had heard Levi speak, and he seemed used to it anyway.

"What do you mean?" I whispered back.

"They didn't put Mom or Dad in here, only the kids," he whispered.

"Why?" I asked.

"Because of our, our gifts," he struggled to say.

"How do you know?" I questioned.

"I saw it coming, I saw it coming all along," he said sadly.

"Why didn't you tell me! Why didn't you tell Mom or Dad!" I yelled.

"You back there, shut up!" Sipes yelled back.

I quickly quieted down.

"Levi! Levi!" I whispered.

He didn't answer.

I need to get us out of here! I thought.

I pulsed.

The whole car shook rapidly.

"Just what we need, another troublemaker!" the man roared.

I pulsed harder.

The seats bounced this time. But I couldn't make my waves as powerful now that I was strapped down.

"Aubrey! Put him to sleep!" he screamed. His voice was grindy, like he'd just ate sand.

Out of nowhere, a sudden drowsiness hit me, my muscles relaxed, and my eyelids started to close. The last thing I saw was a girl with piercing blue eyes staring at me.

CHAPTER 6

Trip to Rebal
Noah Tone

Everything was blurry at first, but then my eyes started to adjust. I felt the straps around my legs and wrists. Everything felt sore.

How long have I been out? I thought.

I looked over. Anna? Were we even still in the car? I looked out the window. A bird flew past, and I could see…clouds? I looked down. It was the ocean! We were on a plane?

"Anna!" I said.

"You're awake!" she said excitedly.

"What do you think?" I replied, annoyed. "Why are we on a plane?" I asked.

"You've been asleep for nearly a day. Four hours ago we boarded. Seth heard them say that we were going to Europe," she said scared.

"Europe?" I repeated.

"Yep, and Seth also heard them say we were gonna go to some sort of school. Rebal International, they said," she answered.

"I'm pretty sure that's in Switzerland," I replied, stunned. "They only let about two hundred students in a year. Only royalty goes there," I explained.

"That's probably what they want everyone to think. Seth also overheard them saying that there were others with gifts like us there. They were training them!" she blurted.

"And I always thought that we were the only ones...," I whispered.

"I know, this is just so much to take in..." She strained herself not to cry. "And Mom and Dad are gone..." A tear slid down her cheek.

"Don't worry. Either someone will find us or I will get us out of here," I reassured her.

"I only wish. Seth also heard them say that no one would find us. They've done this to other kids many other times. And no one's ever figured out," she said, defeated.

"That's impossible! The parents surely would have called the police or looked for their kids. Soon enough someone will rescue us," I said hopefully.

"I hope," she whispered.

"Did Seth hear anything else?" I asked.

Her eyes turned alert. "No, they overheard him talking to us about everything. Then that scary girl made him pass out," she said shakily.

"Are you okay?" I asked.

"I just x-rayed the two guys in front of our seats. They have pistols." She quivered. "Don't do anything stupid!" she warned. "You're the only person that I've been able to talk to for ten hours. Seth, Jesi, and John are asleep," she explained.

"They took Johnny too!" I fumed, enraged.

"Yeah," she answered. "Keep it down, or blondie is going to come back here!" she warned.

I tried to look around for the girl, but the straps kept me still. "This is so unfair!" I said under my breath. "I would like to strap them up, then they'd see how we feel," I said to no one in particular.

"Don't push your luck. These guys are all about the business," she replied.

"All right." I breathed out heavily.

It didn't make any sense. Why did they want us, what did they want to do with us, and why did they take John, my three-year-old brother? He didn't even have a power, as far as I or my parents knew.

"Why did they take Johnny? He doesn't even have a gift," I asked Anna.

"I was confused at first as well, but Seth heard them say that John might have a power too, and a valuable one," she answered.

"No way!" I replied. "If he had a gift, then we would know by now," I fumed.

"I don't think he has a power either," she said.

"But if he did have a power, what would it be?" I asked.

"I don't know, I just don't know," she answered.

The trip continued on long and uncomfortable. They only gave us water to drink but nothing to eat. Anna was looking pale, and all the others continued to snooze away. Suddenly Seth started snoring.

"Aw, come on! How many problems can a private jet face!" Sipes yelled.

"Bring him back up, Aubrey. Snoring is not something that we would like to hear!" he commanded.

"Whatever, Brock," she said, clearly annoyed.

As she walked past me and Anna's seat, she stopped and stared at me. She was about my age, maybe younger. She had sun-colored hair and the purest blue eyes that I'd ever seen.

"Too bad I had to put you to sleep," she said soothingly. "We could have sat next to each other…" A sudden wave of sleepiness hit me. My head slowly started to bend down. I tried to fight it, but it was like she had control over every action and thought I had.

"Stop!" Anna yelled. "Don't do it to my brother again!"

"He may be your brother, but as long as he's around me, he's mine," she shot back at her.

Anna hit me on the head. I barely felt it. "Noah! Fight it!" she screamed.

"Come on, Aubrey. Give the boy a break and do what I told you in the first place!" Brock yelled.

The sleepiness left my body immediately. I shot back to attention, glaring at Aubrey.

"Next time, don't expect me to stop. I have complete power over you when you're around me," she said, smiling.

"Don't expect me to be around you, and the next time you try to do that, I won't be afraid to fight you," I warned.

"Oh, but during training, we'll always be together, and if you as much as touch me, you'll answer Blade," she sneered.

I wasn't going to say anything else. She was actually scary.

"And you," she said in disgust, pointing at Anna. "The next time I put you to sleep, you won't wake up!" She smiled then walked down the aisle.

"I can't stand it when she does that to you guys." She shuddered, stricken with fear. "Do you think she'll keep doing that to us?" she asked me.

"Don't worry, she won't," I promised.

"Good," Anna said, then she leaned against the seat and stared ahead, not daring to fall asleep.

Deep in my mind, I knew I wouldn't be able to keep the promise I'd given my sister. How much hope did any of us have left?

I heard Aubrey's footsteps echo against the floor. As she passed our seat, a shiver went up my spine. *If there were other people with powers at the school, then what powers would they have? Would they all be cruel like Aubrey?* The thought racked me with terror. I knew that not everyone in my family would be able to handle it, especially the younger ones.

I wondered how Jesi hadn't killed them already with his gift. He would have gone all out on them if they'd tried to kidnap him, unless Aubrey helped capture him, then he would be hopeless. I looked through the crack on the side of the seat. I saw steam rising from Jesi's straps and his seat was halfway melted. He must have tried to escape but was too late.

The thought filled me with anger. What have we ever done to deserve this? Why couldn't we all be normal like everyone else? It wasn't fair!

I remembered Ava. Had they captured her too? I hoped not. But she was at the school with me. There was a good chance that she had been captured too.

I tried to think positively. She would be on the plane with us if she was captured.

But I had the feeling that she had been captured too. These people seemed filthy rich. They must have plenty of jets like this one. And this Blade guy, he must be the boss that Brock and Sipes were talking about. He must be even worse than Aubrey if he was running this school. He probably had people kidnapped on his command. The thought of meeting him filled me with inexpressible fear. Did he have a whole army, an evil worldwide organization? Was he a terrorist or a madman? I pushed out those thoughts. I was going crazy.

Suddenly I heard Seth whisper from behind me.

"We're going to land," he said.

"Are we almost there?" I asked.

"Ten minutes away from where we land," he answered.

"Your gift is so helpful," I said.

"I must have looked like a fool snoring away," he said, defeated.

"No, they're the fools. They think that they can get away from whatever they want. But they should know better," I said sternly.

"You should watch what you say, boy," Sipes growled from the seat across from me and Anna.

The plane landed, the tires skidding across the smooth pavement.

I quickly shut my mouth. I started to sweat.

"Blade is more powerful than you can imagine. He has stations, compounds, and schools all around the world," Sipes sneered. "He could destroy the US military," he said confidently.

Brock stepped over, unstrapping me and standing me up. He and Sipes did the same to everyone else. It felt unbelievably good to move freely. We stepped off the plane, the flight attendant checking us for any weapons. Sipes stepped next to me, determined to continue the conversation.

"Lies," I said.

"Ha. Tell that to Blade," he taunted. "I've been taken from my family, forced to work for him. But I can't complain. I'd be punished severely." He sounded defeated too.

We all stepped into a limo, and this time the seats didn't have straps.

"We expect all you kids to have perfect behavior now that we're not babysitting you," Brock ordered.

"Oh, don't worry, I'll take very good care of them," Aubrey said, staring right at me.

"Back off, sunshine," I told her.

"Aubrey, you sit next to me," Brock commanded.

"Aw, you're no fun!" Aubrey joked. Then she turned to me and said, "Next time, honey." I walked away in disgust, sitting next to Sipes.

"Even if Blade did have all that you told me, he should be using his power for good," I replied.

"It's better to believe than to not believe, especially when it comes to Blade," Sipes said seriously. "I should know," he said, staring into space.

It seemed like Sipes didn't like to work for Blade. Maybe he wasn't as bad as I thought. It seemed more like he was forced to do Blade's will.

How many lives had this Blade guy turned miserable? He seemed evil, and I hadn't even met him yet. That's usually not a good sign.

Before I knew it, we were pulling up to a huge building, Rebal International. It had no fences, no watch towers. There wasn't even a road block. This was not how I pictured a place where kidnappers lived.

We pulled into the driveway. It looked like the pavement had just been put down. We all stepped out of the car, Aubrey in the back to keep us in check.

A nurse walked Johnny through the door.

"Hey, where are you taking him?" I asked Brock.

"To the lab, nosy. It's none of your business," he shot at me.

"It is too my business. He's my brother!" I yelled back.

"What do you think you're doing!?" Seth whispered, staring at Brock in terror.

"Best you keep your mouth shut, Tone, or we'll shut it for ya," he threatened.

I forced myself not to run in and save John.

Another nurse lady came up to us. We lined up against the curb, listening to her orders. She walked by each of us, checking each of us off on a clipboard.

The papers dropped next to me.

I pulsed, just hard enough so she grabbed her ears.

I quickly knelt down and grabbed the papers, leaving blank paper in the clipboard in their place.

I took her papers and stuffed them in my pocket. I'd look at them later.

I stopped the ringing in her ears, and she looked around confused.

"Sorry about that, I don't know what came over me," she stammered.

Brock and Sipes eyed each of us suspiciously. I kept a straight face. The nurse turned to Brock and Sipes, and they turned their attention to her.

"Blade will be pleased," she said to Brock and Sipes.

"Thank you, ma'am," Sipes and Brock said in unison.

She walked up to me and said, "Blade wants you to meet in his office. He has taken a special interest in you, Noah Tone."

"Where will my brothers and sister go?" I asked.

Aubrey got in my face, batted her eyelashes, and said, "Oh, they'll be with me."

The nurse pushed Aubrey out of the way. "They will be with me, honey. I'll make sure their all safe," she answered, scared.

What was she scared of, me? I should be the one that's most scared!

Brock grabbed my arm.

"You heard her, let's get going!" he said gruffly. "I want to get my pay!" he growled.

I turned to look at my family one last time. "I'll be back." I reassured everyone.

Brock shoved me through the doors. What I saw was amazing. There was a marble floor and a life-size fossil of a Tyrannosaurus rex. TVs lined the walls, and I saw a parlor and restaurant out of the corner of my eye to the right.

Brock and Sipes led me up a spiral staircase circling the fossil. The staircase had velvet carpet going all the way up. These people were really, really rich. And if they had places like this all around the world, then they must be even richer than the president.

Once we got to the top of the staircase, we walked down the hallway to the right. Paintings, certificates, and photos lined the walls. One of the photos had a picture of…Aubrey! This place may be nice, but it was really weird.

We stopped in front of an elevator. Brock shoved me inside, and Sipes pushed the button to the top floor.

We went up in the elevator for at least a minute, the paneling gold and the interior silver. This place was amazing, but at the same time, somehow, someway, it felt like a prison.

Once the elevator stopped and the door opened, we were met by huge oak doors with elaborate carvings on it, with a gold plate at the top of the door labeled Rebal Headmaster's Office.

Before Sipes even opened the door, it started to automatically open. Gradually, a figure in the middle came into place. He had glossy brown hair, with a gold-and-silver tie and a white suit. His white dress shoes clicked as he walked up to me. He offered his hand.

I carefully took it, half expecting a zap to go up my arm, but nothing happened.

"Hello, my name is Blade Mercantile. We've been expecting you, Noah Tone."

Chapter 7

The Talk
Noah Tone

The way he stared at me felt uncomfortable, like I was an amazing piece of art or jewelry. His smile was taking up nearly half his face, and his teeth were literally shining. His skin was pale, and he looked around twenty years old.

"Come in, Noah. You and I are going to have a talk," he said almost threateningly.

I wanted to crawl under the floor and never come back out. "Yes, sir," I said seriously, acting like everything was normal.

He led me to a mahogany desk, around fifteen feet long and five feet wide. It had four plush leather chairs circling it. There was one seat that was exceptionally larger than the others at the head of the desk. The spacious room around the desk had paintings of all sorts, columns lined everywhere around the room, and a large piano was to the right of the room. To the left stood a huge, flat screen TV, with a velvet couch, and a bearskin rug underneath it. The floor was made of granite.

Beautiful carvings were on everything that was wood, and a fireplace stood underneath the TV. It had to be as big as my house.

How rich could these people get, and how did they get this rich?

I slowly took my seat, taking in the overwhelming surroundings.

"It's beautiful, isn't it?" Blade inquired.

"What's beautiful?" I asked, pretending to act curious.

"Why, my, my room of course." He laughed, a hint of suspicion in his voice. He sounded greedy already.

"What are you going to do with my brothers and sister?" I asked, raising my eyebrows as I said it.

"Why must you go fast in everything you do? Just take it slow and easy, come to the realization that this is where you belong," Blade said triumphantly.

"I don't understand," I said.

"You are very special, Noah. Do you know why you are here?" he questioned.

"Because of our gifts," I said sternly.

"Ah, your gifts, that's what your parents probably want you to call them. They want you to think that you're not powerful, not as capable as you really are," he said bitterly. "But they're wrong, Noah. You can do amazing things," he said, a hint of astonishment in his voice.

"You know my parents?" I asked.

"I knew them well," he said.

"But you're only around twenty. We would know if you met my parents." I seethed.

"Quite the contrary, I am fifty years old, almost fifty-one as a matter of fact," he explained. I stared at him, confused. "Don't judge a book by its cover, Tone. You must know who someone is before you decide who they are for yourself," he said.

"My parents wouldn't be like you. They're good," I said.

"Are you saying that I'm not good?" he asked, pretending to be hurt, but doing a horrible job at it. "I raised your parents, knew them like friends. Why, I trained them," Blade said.

"Your tricks don't work," I fumed. "I know you're lying."

"You can believe whatever you want, but I remember those days vividly," he said, clearly disappointed for some reason.

"You still haven't answered my question. Why did you kidnap us? What do you want us for?" I ordered.

"My, my, there's no getting around it this time!" he joked. "You're like Dr. Parkins, my old friend." He breathed out heavily. "I do wish you don't turn out like him. He had a...sad end."

"Who is this guy?" I asked. "Another evil man like you?"

"You are brave, very brave to insult me...I like that," he said slowly. "Ah, Parkins." He sighed. "He was such a good friend. We fought cancer together, you know. Then he found something, created something that was very amazing, even revolutionary. He found the cure to cancer," he said expectantly.

"More lies. People still have cancer today," I shot back.

"At least he thought it was the cure...," he said sinisterly, his mouth turning into a wicked grin, his eyes turning into slits. "That cure, that...bad medicine, it turned you into this," he said, gestering to me.

"I don't see anything wrong with me," I fired back, even though sweat was beading down my forehead. I knew what he was talking about. He was talking about my gift. *Could he be telling the truth? Could an awry experiment have turned me into this? And what did my parents have to do with it?*

"Your parents, they had powers too, son. They turned you into this," he seethed.

"No! No, it can't be true!" I yelled.

"It's time to face reality, Noah. You never really thought that you just somehow magically manifested your power, did you?" he said, smiling.

"It's your fault!" I screamed. "You made that cure and put it into my parents!" I roared.

"No, Dr. Parkins did. He created the cure. The only thing I did was, well, borrow it," he said, sounding confused himself.

"You're messing with my brain! You're turning me to your side!" I yelled.

"It's your choice whether to join me or not, not mine," he replied sincerely.

I breathed out heavily. I couldn't let him do this to me. I had to give him a taste of his own medicine. Bad medicine.

"You did this to all the other kids' parents. That's why others have powers too." I breathed out heavily.

"Yes, I have had great success. Now the Rebal has at least two hundred teens, children, and toddlers in the organization with powers. We have had great success. Unfortunately, most parents wouldn't cooperate with us stealing their children, so we had to put an end to them, but not before we ran tests on them," he said wickedly. He was nuts. "We do wish we had more children, but your family and Ava's were the last that we know of. And unfortunately both of your parents would not cooperate. They will be put to death," he sneered.

"Noooo!" I screamed. Feeling weaker than ever, I was barely able to hold myself on my seat. I fought back tears. *I still have time. I can rescue the kids, then rescue Mom and Dad,* I thought.

I wiped my eyes then sat straighter. This man, Blade, he had done this to me. He would pay. "You won't get away with this. Someone will stop you," I growled.

"What exactly do you think I intend to get away with? Murdering your parents? Your parents should be the least of your worries," he sneered.

I swallowed. "I don't know what you want to train us for, but I'm guessing that it's not good either," I said.

"Perhaps in your eyes. But in mine, it's only what was destined to happen," he said while standing up. "You see, Noah, we only have so much of the cure. We can only make so many people get powers. Depending on the type of person, medical condition, and health someone is facing, the results always differ. But unfortunately, a ruckus caused Dr. Parkins's papers that have the ingredients and formulas for the cure to get lost, or perhaps destroyed," he said, a hint of disappointment in his voice.

"Why don't you just look for the papers?" I asked.

"We searched every centimeter of the room. Either it was lost or…someone took it. We suspect that one of the parents to the children with powers is responsible for it. That is why we took your parents somewhere else, somewhere that no one will find them," he growled. "I do hope you don't go looking for them," he sighed.

"Then you would make a seemingly unstoppable enemy, me," he said threateningly.

I stared at him, his piercing green eyes feeling like daggers stabbing me.

"Why are you training us?" I asked.

"I'm glad you asked," he said, evidently excited. "Power. Dominance. Taking over the world seemed impossible, until you children came around," he said wickedly.

I tried to comprehend what he was telling me.

"That's right, Noah, we're going to take over…the world," he said, relishing in the thought.

"Even with us that's impossible. Do you not know how much resistance we would be met with?" I asked.

"Oh, I know better than anyone what we're facing, but it seems that even you don't know your own potential," he seethed. "You may be able to destroy buildings and people, but have you ever tried to destroy a tower, a town, a continent?" he questioned.

"Well, I—"

He cut me off. "Exactly. You don't know your own potential," he said seriously. "That's why we train you, so you do know your own potential. We are all about business, Noah. We're serious about taking over the world, more serious than you could understand. Once we have shown everyone what they can do, and once we find the formula for the cure and form a whole army of powers, the world will face something they've never faced before, something they will be too slow to understand. They will face…a *plague of powers*."

His words drilled themselves into my mind. *Could he really take over the world? Was he drunk? Was he crazy?*

"Your power is amazing, Noah, and it only gets more powerful the more you learn about it. It is time to pick a side," he said, desperation in his voice.

"If I go with my family, if I go back home, I could possibly get all my brothers and sisters out of here…but we would be in danger of you constantly…and, and my parents, we would rescue them next! We could get away from you!" I said, realizing what I could do.

"Perhaps, but your chances would be as low as you could possibly imagine. There would be little or no chance of you winning," Blade replied.

"But if I stay with you, you would kill my parents, you would turn my brothers and sisters into your slaves, you, you would make them and me take over the world, kill innocent people…and for what, power? Power that you would gain all for yourself!" I yelled.

"You're smarter than you look, Tone, but I'm afraid you know too much. I cannot afford you to ruin my plans. You will be thrown in with the failures like yourself. They failed to choose wisely," he said, disappointed.

I tried to pulse, but suddenly, a burning pain shot through my whole body. I fell to the floor in a crumpled heap.

All of a sudden, Blade was standing over me. "I am so sorry but so disappointed in you, Noah. Now you will know true pain," he growled.

Everything went black.

Part Two

Chapter 8

Thief of the Cure
Gabe Tone

Gabe struggled against the chains, feeling the grooves in his wrists and ankles where they had been placed. He regretted everything. He regretted taking Noah to the wrestling match, he regretted not looking out for his children better, he regretted not using his gift to save them, but most of all, he regretted not telling them, not telling them that he, their father, had a gift too.

"The kids, the kids, they're gone!" Sara screamed. She had been wailing and crying all day and night. She had gone crazy. He had gone crazy as well, but now all he could think was, *Survive, escape, save the family.*

He should've known Blade would come back. Ever since training he had known that Blade was nuts, crazy, mad. He had trained him to use his powers, but he was using him. He was using everyone. *He was using us for power.*

This was Blade's revenge. He should've known he would come for them. Blade always saw him as the rebellious one, the one who would turn.

A memory suddenly took over.

It was 1997. He was in Rebal International. He had just been kidnapped from his family. He was sitting in a lab chair, strapped down, ready to be tested. He was shivering, not from the cold outside, but from the terror that had been washed over him. He was only seventeen. Nothing made sense. He suddenly saw a cute girl in the chair next to him. She was younger than him. And even though her hair was messed up, she still looked pretty. It was Sara. Little did he know that someday she would be his future wife.

Suddenly the phone rang.

"Hello?" the nurse in the room said into the phone.

"Inform Blade that we're coming and with something very important." The voice was static but still clear.

"I'll inform him right away, but first he needs to know what you're bringing," she said, clearly bored.

"Tell him we have a very special girl named Emma." The voice suddenly paused. "And we have the cure."

The nurse's eyes suddenly widened as big as golf balls.

"I'll inform him immediately!" she said excited. "Blade will be pleased," she added.

"Not a second later. We need to get this experiment going. Blade has taken extreme interest in this project. From now on, it will be a top priority," he said seriously.

The nurse ran out of the room, dropping the phone as she did.

"Ha. Those kids will have no idea what hit them," the voice said on the phone. "No idea." Static.

"I'm scared," the girl next to him whimpered.

"Me too, me too," he said.

Ten minutes later a scary doctor came in with a tray of shots and needles and a mysterious-looking vial of liquid. *It must be the cure,* he thought.

The doctor came up to him first.

"Hold still, Tone," he said gruffly.

He closed his eyes. He could barely feel the cold needle go in his skin.

Suddenly a horrible pain hit him. He started to scream. His muscles were literally growing. He could feel every layer of skin stretching. He stopped screaming. Now he was panting like an animal. He could feel his brain getting bigger. His skull started to ache. Then he directed all his anger on the doctor. He had done this to him. His vision and hearing was blurry. He could hear faint screams and wails. *Clang!*

A pipe came undone.

Clang! Clang! Clang!

Pipes were flying all over the room. One hit the doctor in the side.

"Gahhh!" he screamed, then crumpled to the floor.

His chair suddenly started to float, then the straps somehow came undone. He dropped to his feet, staring right at the doctor, who was looking up at him in terror.

Gabe raised his hand. The bed came up with it, floating in mid-air. He was about to smash it onto the man when a voice startled him.

"Telekinesis, extraordinary," the voice breathed out in bafflement.

Gabe looked up, there. Standing in the doorway was a man with glossy brown hair, a gold-and-silver tie, a white suit, and white dress shoes.

Just then Gabe woke back up from the memory. The rest he couldn't remember.

He didn't dare use his powers for fear that his constraints would give him a heart attack again. The technology they had created was amazing but also gruesome.

The restraints could sense when the prisoner used his or her powers, and every time the person tried to use their powers, a burning pain shot through their entire body, causing a heart attack. Each time they tried to use their power, the worse the pain would become. Gabe was amazed that he hadn't died from the last attack.

It seemed that he would kill himself before Blade got the chance to interview him.

He tucked the papers he had sworn to protect deep into his pants pocket. He couldn't let them find it. Then he would fail his family, then he would fail the world.

CHAPTER 9

Interview Gone Wrong
Gabe Tone

Gabe looked over at Sara, her hair in a tangled mess, her face streaked with tears. She looked the same as day she was captured.

"The kids, we need to find them," she whispered to Gabe.

"I'll do whatever it takes to get us out of here, whatever it takes," Gabe promised.

And he wasn't going to break that promise.

He had to get them out of here now.

Suddenly the doors opened.

The first light they'd seen in days quickly flooded the room. His eyes took a moment to see the figure standing in the doorway.

It was a Rebal guard, definitely not the first he'd seen.

"It's time," the guard told him.

He was surprised that he had survived. Had they been in there for days, weeks, years? It was hard to keep track in pitch-blackness.

"Took you long enough," he said.

"Two days celled and still determined. I'd be astonished if you weren't such a traitor," the guard sneered.

That's the way you handled the Rebal, always act calm, determined, and cool. It's what they hated the most.

He couldn't stand. He could only kneel. If he left his position, then the heart attacks would flood his body.

The guard came over and roughly took the chains off, then before he took off the leg braces, he strapped a band around Gabe's wrist, then with a key locked it into place. He heard the dreadful sound of the lock click then knew there was no turning back. The band applied the same heart attacks the cuffs did if you tried to use your power. If there was one thing he knew, it was that the Rebal took no chances.

He then took off the leg chains then stood him up. He could barely walk after being celled for two days. But he had to act determined. That way he could keep his play going.

"I can stand myself," Gabe said, his voice a croak.

"Suit yourself," he said, letting him go.

At first he was a little wobbly, but then he got used to his upright position and followed the guard out of the cell. Before he left the cell, he stopped and turned back to face Sara.

"We'll be out soon," he reassured her.

As he turned right and walked down a corridor, the guard laughed.

"Good luck with that," he cackled.

He smiled. His plan was working. They thought he had no chance of escape. The only question he had was, *Would they be able to escape me?*

He knew Blade's tricks, tactics, and traps better than almost anyone. After all, they trained him for five years, or should he say sabotaged them for five years.

As we neared the end of the corridor, he saw the familiar-looking metal door of an interrogation room. *This hasn't been the first time I'd been tortured. Every time I stayed strong. I knew Blade couldn't afford to lose me, could he?*

The guard shoved open the metal door, and a sudden gust of cold air hit his body. The room smelled fresh and newly made. He had no idea what compound he was in but had a feeling that it had been built recently. Blade probably had compounds being built as of now. Even he didn't know how he got so rich.

As they entered the room, he saw the torture chair, shiny and new, sitting in the middle of the room. All sorts of attachments had probably been put into it. The thought sent chills throughout his body. He still remembered the screams he heard as a young boy coming from the interrogation room next door. He had nightmares every day because of it.

He was glad he wasn't going to be one of those people.

The guard pushed him farther into the room. Gabe took his time to make them think he was buying time, but he had already formulated a plan. He caught a glimpse of Blade in the far right corner at the top of the room, sitting in a metal chair, a tray full of needles and other torture equipment on a tray to his left.

He looked no different than the first time Gabe saw him. He still wondered if he had plastic surgery.

"Hello, Blade," he said casually.

"Hello, old friend," Blade said in disgust.

"I was wondering when you would change the style of the torture chair. It still looks nice, though," he bluffed, even though he knew that it was the old model in disguise.

"Oh, it's the old girl, all right," Blade sneered. He pressed a button, and spikes protruded from all sides.

Score. His plan was coming together.

"And this time I'll be the one to torture you so I can eliminate any chance of escape. This time you won't get away, Gabe," he growled.

"What are you going to ask me first?" he asked smoothly as the guard strapped him in the chair.

"I'm surprised you're not weeping for your life, but very well, I will ask you my first question," he said, smiling wickedly.

Gabe moved his wrist to the side so the lock was right over one of the spikes along the chair.

"Where is the cure?" Blade said. The whole room fell dead silent.

"I already told you a million times before, I didn't steal it," Gabe said calmly.

"You're just like your son, pushing it past the limit. I won't ask you again. I know you stole it. You turned all the others to your side after you told them my plan. You ruined everything. You are the only person who would dare to take the papers!" he yelled.

"Even if I did take the papers, I would never tell," Gabe said sternly.

"Very well. Let us start the torture." He seethed.

A screen lit up showing a diagram. This was what Blade always did to his victims. He showed them what would happen to them step after step. This usually scared them enough that they would give him whatever he wanted. But he figured out a way around it.

"This is the first phase," he said sinisterly. "We've changed the whole process," he sneered.

No, they couldn't have. Then his plan would be ruined!

Number one showed up on the screen. It showed a dummy sitting in a chair. He couldn't bear to watch. He broke out in a sweat.

The dummy sat there, frozen for about a second, when a lever lowered the feet downward so the feet were bending over the seat.

Wait a minute. This was the same so far. Maybe his plan would work.

Another second passed when suddenly the spikes protruded from the sides, then they started to go round and round the chair like a chainsaw, slicing the feet nearly off. The only difference from the old tortures was that the spikes went back the other way for about another two minutes, adding a double pain to the torture.

It was perfect. Blade had been foolish this time. Gabe had won.

He carefully placed the metal bracelet in front of the spike, waiting for the moment when the torture would start.

"So will you tell me where the papers are or shall the pain start?" Blade threatened.

"No matter how much you torture me, I won't tell you anything, Blade!" he yelled.

Blade's face turned bright red in anger.

"You leave me no choice, Tone," he growled.

The chair started to steam, then as if in slow motion, the spikes sprang to action. Not a millisecond later, they stopped. His band had stopped the turning.

A metal screeching sound filled the room, and the spike snapped the band in half.

He was no longer restrained from using his power. He jumped out of the seat, staring in hatred, right at Blade.

Blade stared at him in horror and amazement.

"You are finished, Blade. What you started will not be fulfilled," Gabe said heroically.

"Even if you do kill me, Dr. Parkins will finish it for me." He smiled.

"Dr. Parkins? He's, he's dead," Gabe stammered.

The guard stood at attention, aiming his gun right at him.

"Think about it, Gabe," Blade sneered.

Gabe saw the guard load his gun, getting ready to shoot, then quickly he forced the gun to aim toward Blade, and the guard fired the gun in surprise, hitting Blade right in the thigh.

"Gahhhhh!" Blade wailed then crumpled to the ground.

"That's for everything you did to me!" he yelled.

Then the metal started peeling off the wall.

He compacted the metal into a huge ball then forced it to shoot at the guard.

The metal ball slammed into the guard with a sickening crack.

He turned to face Blade, who stared up at him in terror.

"You'll pay for this, Tone," he growled.

"No, you will," Gabe replied.

Suddenly the door shot open.

Three teens were standing there. He guessed they had powers.

One of the teen's eyes turned red, then laser shot out of his eyes.

The other girl started a spinning storm of metal, pipes, and chairs to fly at Gabe. He dodged them, but then he felt the laser tear at his shoe. His shoes started to burn, then his foot.

The other boy knelt down next to Blade and put his hand on Blade's back. Blade slowly stood back up. He was healed.

In the midst of a storm of lasers and metal, Blade's and Gabe's eyes met. Blade's face was twisted in hatred. Gabe stared back, a determined look set on his face.

Just as a piece of metal was about to hit Gabe, he blasted everything outward. A chair slammed into the boy with laser eyes, all the metal that hit the girl stuck to her like she was a magnet, and the boy with healing powers got hit in the head with a pipe. He missed Blade. He felt sorry for the kids he had hurt. It wasn't their fault. Blade had brainwashed them, just like Blade had brainwashed him.

The girl took a step toward him, the metal regrouping around her. He couldn't stop Blade now. He had to rescue Sara.

He turned to Blade, ignoring the girl.

"You won't get away with this, Blade!" he yelled.

Blade stood and told the girl, "Finish this traitor!"

She was just about to blast him with metal when Gabe shot upward into the air. He had to rescue Sara then get out of here.

He looked down on the building. He was at least one mile in the sky, Blade and the teens no longer visible. The compound looked small from up there, but it was no compound—it was a lab. He could tell by all the windows and lone buildings surrounding the main building. *What is Blade up to this time?* he thought.

He looked at the forest surrounding the lab. Palm trees and sand were the only thing he could see from there. *Oh no. That can only mean one thing.* He shot into the sky up higher, then with fearful eyes gazed down and saw a vast desert of light-blue water, an ocean. Just what he suspected. They were on an island.

CHAPTER 10

Lockdown
Blade Mercantile

Blade stormed through the hall, not surprised when he was met by a platoon of guards around the corner.

"What are your orders, sir?" the commander asked.

"Put the entire lab on lockdown. Not one guard, soldier, or commander will be off duty! Everybody will be alert and ready for the worst. I'm afraid an uprising has started," he growled.

"Between the guards?" the commander asked.

"I wish it was that, but I'm afraid that a power has broken loose, and a dangerous one," he seethed.

"I will take the report to the command center immediately," the commander replied.

"And get my jet. I feel it is time to leave. No sense in staying in a warzone," Blade said. "Natalie, Jason, come with me," Blade ordered. He could see the swell on Jason's head from the pipe starting to heal. "And get Cole medical help immediately. He is badly injured in the interrogation room due to the loose power," he commanded.

"Yes, sir!" the commander yelled, all his guards standing at attention.

"I believe my time here is done. Make sure my jet is outside ready," he added.

He was just walking away when he remembered. "And I also have a special favor to ask. Tell the scientists in lab room 108 that we need a new torture chair design *without* razor blades," he growled, remembering his failure. "I will make sure that no…mishaps occur in the future," he seethed.

"Yes, sir," the commander replied, an obvious look of confusion on his face.

Blade tugged his tie and swung around, his heels clacking against the tile floor. Once they got outside to the runway, the jet stood there, waiting for them.

"Jason, Natalie, go ahead of me," he ordered.

The kids went in front without hesitation.

Once Blade was about to the top of the steps, he turned and looked out onto the lab.

"You'll pay, Gabe," he sneered.

He boarded the jet then realized, *The lab won't stand a chance against him.* He had never regretted teaching Gabe as much as he did now.

In spite of everything, he laughed. *The lab may not stand a chance against Gabe, but Gabe won't stand a chance against me.*

CHAPTER 11

Total Annihilation
Gabe Tone

Gabe flew down to the roof of the main building of the lab complex, hitting the roof with a thud. Then he concentrated on the section of the roof. In no time at all, a hole appeared.

He couldn't believe that he was using his power finally.

It seemed like a forgotten past, but now that he felt so used to it, it felt so natural.

He jumped through the hole and wasn't surprised when the sound of shots filled the room.

Still, he thought.

Everything and everybody around him froze immediately.

He could see the looks of confusion, anger, and fear still plastered onto the guards' faces.

He knew he didn't stand a chance against Blade, with the other powers with him, but knowing Blade, he probably had already escaped the fight like a coward.

He ran past the guards. He saw bullets floating in midair all around him. He could only use his power for so long before he tired. He had to end this quick and destructively.

He concentrated on the wall to his right.

Crush, he thought.

A grinding sound filled the air, then the wall flew to the right, crushing anything in its path. He heard screams and wails. He felt guilty again. These people were forced to work for Blade, but it was the only way, his only way to get out. There had to be sacrifices.

He looked at the wall he had destroyed, a huge hole in its place. Beyond that was jungle. He had already destroyed half the main lab.

He couldn't do the same to the other wall. Sara was over there.

He raced down the hallway to the left, feeling a sense of hope as the cell doors reflected the sunlight. He raced down the cell doors, 10, 15, 17, 30, 37! He'd found their cell, cell number 37.

He concentrated on the cell door.

Disappear, he thought.

The cell door suddenly was gone, and in its place was a frail lady cringing at the sunlight.

Sara.

Her face was streaked with tears, and she was quietly sobbing.

"Please don't take me," she whimpered.

"Sara, it's me!" he replied brightly.

"Gabe, is, is that you?" she asked, squinting at him. "I must be hallucinating!" she said scared. "I'm going crazy!" she wailed.

"No, Sara, it's really me, it's really me," he said gently.

She looked down, crying for joy.

"Don't worry, I'm going to get you out," Gabe reassured her, angry at the Rebal for what they had done to her.

He concentrated on the chains.

Break, he thought.

A metallic sound erupted. *Pink!* All four of the locks snapped.

Sara stood, wobbly at first as well, then felt her wrists, and for the first time since they'd been captured smiled.

Gabe ran to her, and they embraced, her head on his shoulder, sobbing.

"Thank you," she whispered.

Bam! Bam! Bam! Gunfire erupted on the left side of the hall.

He ducked into the cell with Sara.

"Rrrr," he growled, feeling the bullet groove on his arm. It had just nipped him.

Sara looked at the cut, then her expression turned to anger. She closed her eyes, pressing her hands to the floor.

Vines started to overgrow the place immediately.

The cell door was now a mass of vines and trunks.

"It'll hold them off for a while. They are probably tangled up as we speak," she said, serious as ever. She was back.

He smiled. The team was back together.

"Well, the labs surrounding the building are our only problem now," Gabe replied, him arm stinging.

"Here," she said, touching his arm. Vines started to intertwine around the cut, making a natural Band-Aid. "This will help," she spoke softly.

He stood and looked at the wall of their cells.

Disappear, he thought again. The wind started to whip their faces, and he opened his eyes. The jungle was straight ahead. They were free.

They sprinted toward the jungle as fast as they could, Gabe blasting away any guards and Sara pulling them into the ground with quicksand any time they were faced with resistance.

They were almost there when a sudden voice spoke out.

"Halt!" it roared.

Suddenly soldiers and guards appeared out of the trees and bushes, around two hundred of them. He and Sara turned around. About another one thousand were behind them. They were surrounded.

"Surrender or die!" the head of the soldiers by the jungle ordered.

Gabe turned to Sara.

"Annihilate?" Gabe whispered.

She nodded her head. "Annihilate," she replied.

She bent toward the earth, touched it, and closed her eyes.

The earth started to tremble. Waves of earth started to roll outward from Sara. Gabe had to fly toward the air so he wouldn't trip.

He looked downward. Soldiers and guards were struggling against the waves of earth, now as tall as him.

He boomed with the loudest voice he could muster, "No, surrender or you will die." All the soldiers' faces turned frightened.

"Attack!" the commander screamed.

The waves burst to the size of a tsunami. Men were flying hundreds of feet into the sky, tossed like rag dolls by Sara.

He looked at the complex. He'd controlled stuff bigger than it was before.

Gabe concentrated on the whole complex.

Lift, he thought.

A deafening *screee* filled the air as the building was torn out of the ground, the cement falling and crushing any survivors that were running out of the lab.

Gabe lifted the whole lab above his head. He looked down. The waves were getting smaller, Sara was getting tired, but there was still a large group of about five hundred men huddled around where the tsunami failed to reach. They would surround her.

Gabe aimed the gigantic building right above the group of men. Sweat beading down his forehead, his arms began to limp. He had to act now.

Gabe concentrated on the men.

Crush, he thought.

The building soared down. Gabe saw the men look up in horror at the building flying down at them for a split second, then they were crushed underneath a million tons of metal and stone.

Foom! The impact sent a shockwave through the earth. What stood in place of the once-shining lab now was a huge crater, barren and lifeless. There were no survivors.

A vine started to rise into the air. There was someone on it. It was Sara.

She came to his level in the sky and looked him straight in the eye. It stayed like that for about thirty seconds when she spoke up.

"You could have killed me!" she yelled.

"Hey, at least they are out of the way," he replied.

She rolled her eyes. "You could have at least given them a fighting chance!" she shot back.

They both laughed.

"Let's get down to ground level. I don't feel great after lifting that whole lab above my head," Gabe said hoarsely.

"I don't feel too good either, but where will we go?" she asked.

"We'll figure that out later," he said.

She let him onto the vine, then they declined back to the ground, wind whipping in their faces.

She led them into the jungle, at least a mile from the lab.

"Why did you take us so far away from the lab?" Gabe asked after they reached the jungle floor.

"I never want to see or go back to that place ever again," she said in terror.

"Me neither, me neither," he replied.

"Now there's just one thing we need to do," she said.

"And what's that?" Gabe asked.

She replied determined and in a stern tone, "Rescue the kids."

Part Three

Chapter 12

Dreaded Report
Blade Mercantile

"Sir, the entire Floreana Lab Complex is…gone," the hoarse voice over the phone replied.

"And why, may I ask, did this happen?" Blade said in disgust, although he had the feeling that he knew already.

"It was not due to something, sir. It was due to someone," the voice said almost in astonishment.

"And who, may I ask, did this?" he growled, feeling anger flowing through his every cell.

"We have reports from the few survivors that clearly state that this was the doing of Sara and Gabe Tone. Changes in the earth's crust, landscape change, and reports of telekinesis back up our evidence of the suspects," he said quickly and anxiously.

"What report chopper are you?" Blade breathed out heavily in annoyance.

"Four-three-two, sir," the voice replied without hesitation.

"Report to my command center immediately to discuss this event with Parkins. He'll deal with this one," Blade replied.

"Yes, sir," the voice said.

He hung up and dialed a different number.

"Yes?" another voice said immediately.

"Hello, Dr. Parkins," Blade replied.

"Ah, Dr. Blade! It's been a while, old friend," Parkins answered brightly.

"We seem to have had a total annihilation at the Floreana Lab Complex," Blade replied darkly.

"You mean it was destroyed?" Parkins replied, confused.

"It seems so," Blade answered in disgust.

"But it was just made!" Parkins roared.

"That is what seems to be so disappointing about it," Blade sneered. "And worse, someone destroyed it," he growled.

"How could we have let this happen!" Parkins yelled from the other side of the phone.

"Oh, I can assure you it won't happen again," Blade sneered. "Report this to your command center. Your lab, your problem," he said.

Blade hung up and slammed his phone down on his desk.

"And I have a promise for you too, Gabe, you won't destroy anything that belongs to me!" he said to himself. "Or next time, I'll destroy you!"

He got out of his chair and briskly walked to the door, slamming it behind him.

CHAPTER 13

Cellmates
Noah Tone

"Noah!" a voice called out.

My eyes slowly opened, and a blurry set of bars formed in front of me. A cold, wet a drop of water fell on my forehead, and I was shivering.

I looked up and saw a familiar face across the room. She had long brown hair and a blue shirt, the same I'd seen at the school.

"Ava?" I said quietly.

"Oh! Are you okay?" Ava asked.

I sat up and groaned. "Yep, good as I'll ever be."

A sudden pain hit my heart. I grabbed my chest and whimpered.

"Those stupid bands!" she cursed. "As if the people here could get any meaner!" she said in anger.

"No, it's not the band. I think Blade did it," I croaked.

"But Blade can't hurt your heart," Ava said.

"He sure can," a voice from the cell next to me boomed. "He's done it to me plenty of times. Blade has powers too," he growled.

"No way," Ava shot back. "I would know."

"Huh, a newbie, eh?" the voice laughed.

Ava's face turned red hot. "I may not know a lot about this place, but at least I respect manners!" she yelled.

"No, he's right," I said. "It would only make sense if he did."

"Whatever," Ava huffed in frustration.

"What's your name?" I asked the guy next to my cell.

"Zack, Zack Gupta," he answered.

"So, Zack, do you have a power?" I asked.

"Everyone down here does. We're failures, the kids who weren't good enough," he said gruffly.

"So what's your power?" I asked.

"Superstrength," he said, almost bored.

"And that's not good enough for Blade!" I almost yelled.

"He means were the ones who wouldn't cooperate," Ava explained in annoyance.

"You met Blade too?" I asked Ava.

"Enough to know that he's psycho, if that's what you want to know," she replied.

"She's right," Zack added. "He may be right about taking over the world, but he's still as nuts as, well, a bag of nuts." He laughed.

"What if the Rebal can hear you?" I said, scared.

"Oh, they don't care about us. They only keep us so they can run tests. We're like dogs or something," he assured us, even though it didn't really lift my spirits at all.

"Why don't you, like, bend the bars or something and get us out of here!" I yelled at Zack.

"You see those bands Ava was talking about?" he asked.

"Yeah," I said, suspicion in my voice.

"If you dare use your power, these bad boys will give you a heart attack like Blade, only not as bad, but don't think it'll feel good!" he warned.

The thought made me cringe in fear. One heart attack was enough for me.

"How long have I been out? I asked.

"Nearly two days. I couldn't stop watching you to see if you'd wake up," she said, scared.

"Ha! Love at first sight!" A voice next to Ava's cell laughed.

"Shut up already, Morri!" Ava screamed.

"You are telling me," Morri put in.

Ava rolled her eyes.

"You'd better get used to being down here, honey, 'cause there's no going back up!" Morri said. Like she was a villain or something.

"How long have you been down here?" I asked.

"For as long as I can remember, really," Morri said, defeated.

"Ohh." I nearly toppled over. "I can't do it!" I wailed.

"Oh, stop whining!" the voice to the other side of Ava yelled in annoyance.

"Who are you?" I asked.

"Jane," the voice replied, now shy for some reason.

"What's your power?" I asked Jane.

"I can turn invisible," she said slowly.

"That's really cool. That could come in handy a lot," I said.

"I know, right," Ava added. "That's what I told her, but she thinks her power is dumb," she said sadly.

I looked over at Jane. She had the darkest hair I'd ever seen and big brown eyes with tan skin. I decided not to push it about her power.

"I never asked you about your power, Morri. What can you do?" I questioned.

"I was kicked out because my power was useless, according to the Blade, at least. I can remember information I find out and literally download it into my brain. I'm like a living computer," she said. She had dirty-blond hair, shortly cut, and pale skin. Her eyes were almost amber.

"That could be really useful," I replied.

"Not if you're taking over the world," she smirked.

"Oh, I see," I answered.

A voice next to my cell made me jump.

"And of course, the most awesome power is last!" he said, annoyed.

"Who, who are you?" I stammered.

He laughed at my sudden reaction.

"Jayce Smith," he said coolly.

"And…" I started.

"I have, drumroll please! Super speed!" he said heroically.

"What a bragger," Ava commented.

I couldn't see what Jayce or Zack looked like because they were on the other side of my wall, so I just asked more questions.

"So you can, like, be a race car?" I asked.

"Oh, no, a jet!" he yelled, obviously full of himself.

"Uh, okaaay," I said.

We sat there in silence for about another hour when I said, "So what goes on down here?"

"It stinks, if you didn't notice already," Morri said in disgust.

"I haven't been here long enough to really know," Ava said.

"The only time people really come in is when they are taking you to the lab or to give you food," Zack explained.

I suddenly noticed how hungry I was. My stomach was growling. I had to have lost a lot of weight by now.

"When do they bring food?" I asked anxiously.

"When they feel like bringing us food," Jayce laughed.

"Do you like it down here?" I asked Jayce.

"It's better than being up there," Jayce said, suddenly very quiet.

I was about to say something else but then saw Morri signaling for me to stop.

"I wish they let us be in one cell altogether. That would be more humane," Jane said shyly.

"Me too," Ava sighed.

"Gross! I wouldn't want to share a cell with the guys, even if they got better food," Morri commented.

Everyone started to laugh. Everything was better with people you knew, even in jail.

"So are there any other people here?" I asked.

"There are two more cell joints. The one to my right is for people without powers, criminals, if you'd say. And the ones to the left go by age group. We are in the fifteen to eighteen section," Zack replied. How did he know so much about this place?

"How many other age groups are there?" I questioned.

"There is a ten to fourteen group, a five to nine group, and a zero to four group," Morri said.

"The older you get, the worse the conditions are for you. The zero to four group is empty," Jayce explained.

"The five to nine group is too. That's because it's easier for Blade to turn and manipulate younger kids to his side," Jane added.

"Know-it-all," Jayce shot at her.

"What are you gonna do, zoom around in circles and hope she dies?" Zack joked.

Jayce just huffed in frustration.

"Do you think my brothers and sisters are celled?" I asked.

"I depends on how old they are, as Jane just explained," Ava replied.

I broke out in a sweat. Could Johnny, Jesi, Seth, Levi, and Anna all be with Blade? No, it couldn't be true.

"I never asked you about your family," Ava said. "How many brothers and sisters do you have?" she asked.

"I have four brothers, John, Jesi, Seth, and Levi. John is three, Jesi is six, Seth is ten, and Levi is thirteen. I have one sister, Anna. She's twelve," I explained.

"Holy moly!" Jayce yelled.

"John, Jesi, and Seth probably didn't turn against Blade, bud," Zack said sorrily.

"Hopefully Levi and Anna turned against Blade though," Morri said, trying to lift my spirits.

I felt queasy. *Why, why me! I was the only person who could save them, and Blade, evil Blade, had turned them to his side! I couldn't bear the thought of fighting them to get them back. It was too much, too much!*

"Noah, are you all right?" Jane asked.

"I wish I could say I was," I said, looking into space.

"I'm so sorry, Noah," Ava whispered.

"We need to get out," I said. "Now."

CHAPTER 14

The Plan

"Uh, how?" Morri said, annoyed. "I've been here, for, I don't know, my whole life!" she yelled.

"You said they took us to the lab every once in a while and they bring us food, right?" I asked Zack.

"Yes," Zack said anxiously.

"Do they ever open the cell doors when they bring food?" I asked.

"No, only when they take us to the lab," Jane said, now hopefully.

"Bingo. That's our ticket out," I said.

"Now I like where this is going!" Jayce beamed.

"So, boss, what's the plan?" Ava said in determination.

"I don't think you're gonna believe this, but this might actually work!" I beamed, hope in my voice.

"I already know I'm not gonna like it," Morri smirked.

"We'll see about that," I replied.

Chapter 15

Jailbreak
Noah Tone

"Everyone set?" I asked.

All the girls gave me a thumbs-up.

"How about you guys?" I asked Zack and Jayce.

"Ready as I'll ever be!" Jayce replied.

"Just give me the word," Zack growled, popping his knuckles.

We were lucky that Zack was going to the lab or else the plan wouldn't work. I felt like I was a ray of sunshine in this cell hallway. Hope was finally coming, maybe.

The door in the hall clicked. *Right on time,* I thought.

A loud creak filled the room, followed by heavy footsteps.

The guard walked past, his belt jangled with countless gadgets. A pistol, grenades, cuffs, tear gas, a club, and…keys! A whole chain full of them! The plan was coming along perfectly.

"Zack Gupta," the guard sneered.

"Over here," Zack replied.

The guard stepped in front of his cell and stuck a key in the lock. *Click!* The guard opened the door. A rusty screeching sound filled the room.

"Time to go," the guard ordered.

Zack stood up and walked out of his cell. His footsteps were heavy. He stepped next to the guard. He was big and broad shouldered. Underneath his shirt, muscles rippled. You could say he had superstrength without his powers. He had tan skin and brown buzzed hair.

"Are you sure it's my turn?" Zack questioned. "I already went last week."

"Uh, are you sure?" the guard asked.

"Positive," Zack replied.

"Well, I was given orders, young man. And I intend to follow them," the guard sneered.

"Wait!" I shouted.

"What now?" The guard roared. "Do you want me to clean your cell?"

"No, it's just that I found the papers for the lab. You must have dropped them. It says that I'm supposed to go!" I yelled.

The guard looked confused then walked over to my cell but kept a wary eye on Zack.

He turned his back to Zack and turned toward me.

"Give me the papers," he ordered.

I was so glad that I had taken the papers from the nurse's clipboard. Anything could come in handy.

I took the papers out of my pocket and ruffled through the papers in the corner of the cell. Anna, Seth, Me.

I stuffed all the other papers in my pocket.

"Hurry up!" the guard yelled.

I scrambled over to the bars and handed the guard the papers. He started to read them.

I looked around the guard while he was occupied and eyed Zack.

He gave me a thumbs-up. He'd gotten the keys off the guard's belt.

The guard looked up at me. "These are the wrong papers, sneaky. They say they took you to the lab on August thirteenth. Today's the seventeenth!" he growled.

"I'll deal with you later," he sneered at me as he stepped in front of Zack.

"Follow me. We are going to the lab. Now," he ordered Zack.

As Zack was walking down the hall, I saw him unlock his bracelet quietly. Yes! It was going to work!

When the guard stopped at the door, he reached down to his belt for his keys.

"Wait, where are my ke—"

Thunk! Zack punched him in the stomach.

The guard flew into the door on the opposite wall with a loud bam.

Zack wasn't lying. He had super strength.

"Oh, yeah!" I yelled. We fist bumped.

"Uh, are you forgetting about us?" Morri asked, annoyed.

"Oh, sorry," I said.

Zack walked over to Morri's cell and unlocked it.

Morri came out, her normal self as usual.

She yawned. "Next time, I expect some food and dessert once you get me busted out!" she joked. Then she said quietly, "Thank you."

"Don't mention it," Zack said.

Next we walked to Ava's cell. Zack gave me a key then walked over to Jane's cell with the rest of the keys.

I bent down and unlocked Ava's cell. Not a second after the lock clicked, Ava jumped out and wrapped me in a hug. I was so surprised I didn't get the chance to react.

She let go of me and wiped a tear from her cheek.

"Thank you, Noah. I've been wanting to get out of there forever, I feel so…free," she said in amazement.

"I know what you mean," I said.

We locked eyes. About a minute later she spoke up.

"Noah, I, I've been wanting to tell yo—"

"Zack!" Jane screamed.

Me and Ava spun around.

Jane and Zack were hugging and kissing each other all over. Wait, were they boyfriend and girlfriend?

"Awkward!" Jayce mouthed from his cell.

"Hey, Zacky, could you, like, ya know?" Jayce pointed to his lock.

Zack broke away from the kiss with Jane and turned to Jayce.

"Perfect timing," Zack said in annoyance.

He knelt down and unlocked Jayce's cell door.

Jayce zoomed out.

"Now unlock my bracelet. I've been dying to get more speed!" he begged Zack.

"Boy, for you it's like a drug!" Morri laughed.

"Jayce is right," I turned to Ava. "We can get on about our reunion later. We still have a jailbreak to get done," I ordered Zack.

"Right," Zack said then walked to each of us and unlocked our bracelets, each of them falling to the floor.

"We should keep the bracelets and definitely the keys," Morri said. "They could come in handy."

"Each of you keep your own bracelets. We'll use them when we need to," I said sternly.

Each of us picked our bracelets back up. I handed Ava hers.

When I handed it to her, she grabbed my hand and squeezed it.

I turned to her and smiled, then said, "Let's get out of here!"

Everyone cheered.

Alarms started blaring. No, they must have seen the cameras.

"Security breach in the third section cells! I repeat! Security breach in the third section cells!" a voice screeched.

I turned the volume to nothing, but not in time. Every guard and soldier knew that we had escaped. We had to act fast.

Everyone turned to me.

"Zack, get us out of here!" I yelled.

Zack sprinted into my cell. We all followed. We couldn't be caught in here. We just couldn't.

Zack grabbed the metal wall and peeled it away, revealing a hole that led to a room filled with crates and shipping boxes that were piled high like mountains.

Morri was right. Behind the cell walls was the storage room, even though the storage room was more like the size of a movie theater.

We scampered into the room, running past rows and rows of boxes and crates. We stopped at a crate that was about the size of a raft.

"This will be good," I said.

Zack pried open the lid with his bare hands and pulled out a rope.

"Would you imagine our luck, it's a box of foresting equipment!" Morri beamed as she read the label on the box.

Zack threw everything out, keeping an ax, a pick, tents, and flashlights.

"Why would the Rebal have a storage box full of foresting equipment?" I asked.

"Who knows." Ava shrugged.

"They always have vacations. They go to places like China and Hawaii," Zack said. "I'm guessing that this is for a camping trip," Zack exclaimed.

"Well, guess they won't have a camping trip now!" I laughed.

Everybody except me hopped into the box. Zack tied the rope through two holes in the front of the box. Jayce stepped in between the rope.

"Just tell me when and I'll step on the gas!" Jayce yelled.

Just then, voices erupted on the other side of the storage room. A flashlight shined on us.

"Over there!" the guard yelled.

Gunfire sprang up immediately.

Crack! Splint! The bullets were ripping up the box.

"Hurry, Noah!" Ava screamed.

I stared at the wall blocking our way out.

I pulsed the hardest I'd ever in my life.

I started to glow green. The sound waves were so powerful you could literally see the eerie green glow of the waves rippling throughout the room. I'd never felt so powerful in my life.

The wall shot out of existence, the remnants circling toward me like a black hole. It was horrifying and amazing at the same time. I couldn't believe what I was doing.

I turned around and shot the remainders of the wall, bricks, wood, and metal at the opposite side of the room, at the guards.

I used the sound waves to create a shield around my friends so that the objects would bounce off the crate and then my friends.

Piles and mountains of crates and boxes toppled over. An avalanche of debris crushed anything in its path.

The guards screamed and cried out as the mountains of storage toppled toward them.

Craaash! The sound of wood splinting, brick smashing, and metal crashing filled the air. I turned down the volume for my friends.

When the smoke cleared, everyone turned and stared at me in astonishment.

"Well, now's our chance!" I said then hopped into the front of the crate. "Jayce, go!" I yelled.

I suddenly flew into Ava, gripping onto the sides of the crate for my dear life. I cautiously looked behind us. A huge hole gaped in the once-gleaming crown jewel Rebal International. Now it looked like a bombing raid had passed over it.

I smiled. Hopefully Blade had learned his lesson. Soon the place that we'd suffered was miles from us, only a speck in the distance. I looked toward the horizon. A city started to materialize in front of us.

"Geneva," Morri breathed out. "I saw it on a vacation magazine once. It's one of the biggest cities in Switzerland."

Jayce started to pant. Sweat was beading down his forehead. I couldn't believe how fast he was running. He wasn't kidding. He was a jet. But even he, like all of us, got tired after a while of using our power.

"Hey, you can slow it down, big guy!" I yelled over his pounding footsteps. The wind was whipping into my face, and I had to move my hair out of my eyes to see his expression.

His long blond hair was wet and plastered against his pale skin even though he must've been going five hundred miles per hour. I was starting to get sick and dizzy too even though I wasn't even driving.

He started to decrease in speed and slowly but surely. He came to about the speed on a highway.

"Goodbye, Rebal. Now to Geneva!" Jayce panted.

"To Geneva!" we all chanted.

Chapter 16

The Search
Noah Tone

The crate bounced still as Jayce rocketed us toward Geneva. I was surprised that the crate hadn't splintered into a million pieces already, I looked behind me and saw Ava's stunned expression, her hair streaked and protruding in all different directions from the wild ride.

She sucked in a breath and said, "How did you do that?" She gasped, looking at me like I was a Japanese kamikaze or something.

"Do what?" I asked.

"What do you mean what! You just turned nearly a fourth of Rebal International to rubble!" she yelled.

"I was just trying to protect us," I said slowly.

A smile started on her face, then Zack peered out from the back of the crate.

"That was awesome, bro!" he cried.

All the others joined in telling crazy stories of what happened and how cool it was that we escaped Blade. All right, maybe we did exaggerate a little, but so what, we were free. And we had a whole lot of opportunity ahead of us and a lot of choices to make.

"So, like, now what?" Morri asked.

I remembered my brothers and sister, my parents. We had to rescue them. But now was not the time to tell them about it, not now that we'd just escaped the Rebal and Blade. I would let them get settled first, then I'd tell them about it.

"I'll tell you what we'll do next after we get settled," I replied.

"Why not now?" Jane asked.

"Now is not the time. You'll understand better once we are ready to talk," I said nervously, hoping they'd buy it.

Ava looked at me with a sad expression.

I turned around and sucked in a breath. I suddenly felt a hand on my shoulder.

"It's about your family, isn't it?" Ava said sadly.

"I said I'd tell you guys when we are settled," I said, not looking back.

"Oh, so now it's all about you, huh?' Morri shot at me.

"What do you want us to do, rescue your parents?" I yelled as I looked back at her.

Morri suddenly looked hurt.

Jane glared at me. "Her parents could have been killed by Blade, Noah!" she shouted.

"Come on, guys, we can figure something out when we get to Geneva!" Zack roared, putting all of us to silence.

I turned back to facing the front. The city lights now didn't fill me with comfort. I couldn't believe I had been so unthoughtful, so mean to hurt Morri like that. I was supposed to make the team stronger, not split it apart.

"I know how you feel," Ava whispered, careful to make sure that the others didn't hear her. "Blade took my parents too. I don't even know if they're alive or not. I cried for them every night in my cell because Blade told me if they wouldn't listen, they would be killed. I'm scared he wasn't lying." She shuddered.

I looked back and saw that she was crying.

I took her hand and said, "Don't worry, we'll rescue mine and your parents. Trust me," I reassured her.

"What about Blade, he'll come back for us, won't he?" she said in fear.

"Oh, he's probably searching for us already," I said, looking back at the ever rolling hills. "But he'll have to get past me first," I growled.

I looked back toward Ava, but she had her head down on my shoulder. She was asleep. I was tired too. Everyone was. I felt a strong need to protect everyone, no matter the cost, especially Ava.

Blade was still out there, and if Sipes was right about him, he never forgives, and he never forgets. We have escaped him for now. But we weren't safe. We never would be until we put an end to Blade once and for all.

"Were nearing the city. Should we stop now?" Jayce asked. I'd forgotten that he was the one getting us to safety.

"Sure," I replied.

The cart lurched to a stop, flinging all of us forward a bit.

Ava slowly took her head off my shoulder.

"It's time to get off," I whispered to her.

She stretched and got to her feet. Stepping out of the cart, I followed along with her, along with the others.

I looked at everyone's tired and exhausted faces.

"We've got to find a place to stay the night," I said.

"Agreed, but where?" Zack asked, helping Jane out of the cart.

Ava stood next to me and looked at me for an answer. I looked at everyone else, everyone else except Morri, that is. I still hadn't gotten over the argument.

Everyone looked at me for an answer, but it never came.

"I remember a place," Morri spoke up. "I have a friend who I remember since I was three. He escaped the Rebal, too. He worked for Blade until he figured out the truth like all the rest of us did." She squinted, as if trying to remember something on a test. "His name was...Reece, yeah, he was Reece," she finally ended.

"Uh, so, could you take us to him?" Jayce asked.

"I don't know where he went, but he did say he was going to Geneva. He, he tried to rescue me but couldn't...The Rebal were after him," she breathed out.

"We are luckier than a leprechaun to have your power, Morri," Jane said.

Morri turned and walked the opposite direction of where me, Ava, and Jayce were standing.

"Where are you going?" Ava called after her.

"Where else would we start to look for Reece?" she replied without looking back.

We traveled throughout Geneva, the city bustling with activity at every corner. The smells of noodles were everywhere. Corner shops with unidentifiable names were on every corner. Baguettes and bread shops were in countless places. European style was as real as I'd read in books. It was like I'd stepped through a time machine. Most buildings were cobblestone or brick. A few towers and complexes jutted out every once in a while, but European style was at its prime here.

How would we ever find one person in this whole city? I wondered.

"How about we get something to eat!" Zack yelled over the noise of the crowd.

"We don't have money," Jane said.

"Jayce can fix that." Zack grinned.

A wicked smile crossed Jayce's face as he let the words sink in. "Right away," he replied gladly.

In the moment it took me to blink, Jayce was back with a wallet.

"You stole money!" Ava yelled.

"No one will figure it out. Cameras are too slow to catch me."

Me, Jane, Morri, and Ava exchanged glances.

"Whatever, Blade steals money all day!" I replied.

Everybody cheered.

"Where are we going to eat?" Morri asked. It seemed like she'd gotten over the argument.

"I think I know just the place." Ava smiled, looking across the road toward a restaurant.

Le Chat-Batte was great. I had spaghetti and rolls, while Zack and Jane got potatoes and fettucini, Ava got angel hair noodles with a Sprite, and Jayce ordered ten Pepsis. The run had taken everything out of him, at least that's what he said.

Morri stayed in a corner, looking toward the ground. I didn't know if she was still mad about the argument or just didn't want to eat. More likely the first.

I couldn't help but feel sorry for her. Blade not only was crazy but he was a monster too. Someday he would pay, and I would be sure to make that day very soon, if possible anyway.

Morri's eyes suddenly widened.
"Guys," she said.
We all turned toward her, our expressions anxious.
"We found Reece," Morri breathed out.

Chapter 17

Reece
Noah Tone

"What?" I asked, not sure I heard what she said.

She didn't answer, just ran toward a table and wrapped her arms around a tall man. He was in the booth across from us, and they were causing a scene. Half the restaurant was staring at them.

I sighed and stood up.

"C'mon, guys, let's go see what this is all about," I said.

We walked toward where Morri was, the man eyeing us suspiciously as we trotted next to him and Morri.

"Who are you?" he asked, Morri finally parting from him.

He had a brown tux on and black shades. He was around six seven, had darkly tanned skin, and had a goatee on his long chin. His face and body were thin, and he looked somewhat like a spy.

"I should be asking, who are you?" Jayce replied.

"Morri, bring him outside," I ordered.

Reece suddenly shot out of his seat.

"I'm not moving anywhere until I get an explanation!" he growled at me.

"There's no time. C'mon, Reece," Morri explained.

Reece glanced back and forth between the group and Morri.

He sighed and said, "All right, I trust you, Mor."

He then stood and said, "But I'm leading the way."

We followed Reece to a black van. He opened the door for us, and we crammed into the van. Morri sat up front with Reece.

The door on the front opened, and Reece stepped into the driver's seat.

"Where do you think he's taking us?" Ava whispered beside me.

"Somewhere safe," I replied.

She looked at me for assurance.

"Hopefully," I added.

We had driven around for about an hour. Jane, Jayce, and Ava were asleep already. I couldn't blame them, though. It had been a long day. I wanted to doze off as well, but I still felt that I had the responsibility of protecting the team.

"Morri told us that your place was in Geneva," I told Reece.

"That's what I wanted everyone to think," he replied. "And basically I am in Geneva, only in the outskirts, though." He chuckled. "Blade's been looking for me for ten years! Imagine that! And the funniest part is, he didn't even find me yet!" He laughed.

I just looked at him in amazement. He had avoided Blade for ten years! Was Blade still looking for him?

"I wish somebody could stop him," I said.

"Somebody can," he replied.

"Oh yeah? Who then?" Zack yelled at Reece.

"The Tripartite," Reece growled.

"What's that?" Morri said.

"Like me, there were others, scientists, who saw Blade's plan and that all he wanted was power. Like me, they were smart enough to escape, with half of the Rebal power behind them. Blade doesn't even know they're working against him. He just thinks the scientists left to start on a project to gain profit in the Americas and Canada," he mumbled.

"Whoa. So, like, these people are working against him…behind his back," I breathed out.

"Pretty much," Reece responded.

"It's too risky. If Blade figured out, it would be a civil war, between the Rebal themselves," Zack put in.

"That's what the Tripartite want, a war to end Blade's power. There are ten scientists, each a leader over a facility or compound. But there's one man who commands them all from the headquarters deep in the heart of the US, in Kansas. His name is Dr. Parkins. But even he doesn't have as much power as Blade, Blade's the dictator of the Rebal, the tyrant. If it wasn't for the cure, he wouldn't be in power," Reece seethed.

"I don't understand," I said.

"You see, the beginning of the Rebal started when twelve scientists created a corporation called the Reballion. Each decided to put forward a new project, a certain project for each scientist. Dr. Easton, from Alberta, chose mineral mining to set forward. Dr. Mill, from Washington, DC, chose warfare production. Dr. Ray, from Greece, chose electric corporation. Dr. Chase, from China, chose to study space exploration. Dr. Ibal, from Peru, chose refineries. Dr. Drake, from Russia, chose oil production. Dr. Batali, from Iraq, chose technology. Dr. Gratis, from Egypt, chose water purification. Dr. Hills, from Britain, chose pollution control. Dr. Trove, from Australia, chose border crossing. Dr. Parkins, from the US, chose trade. And finally, Dr. Blade, from Switzerland, chose medical studies. Because of the cure, his power increased so much so that the other scientists feared that he would take control of the whole corporation. Blade alone already owned half of the profit of the corporation. He was hungry for power. The others, led by Dr. Parkins, decided there was no choice but to get rid of him. They created a cover-up trip to the Americas and Canada, telling Blade that they would set up facilities over there to gain more profit for the organization, but really, they are setting up air bases, naval docks, and army compounds. They are preparing for war," he replied.

"How are they so rich and powerful?" Zack asked Reece.

"Well"—every ear turned toward his voice, and I even increased his volume so I wouldn't miss a word—"every single scientist did something that's never been done. Each of them became the most successful and most powerful organization in their field. Combined, their profit is beyond measure. They could create their own empire," Reece explained.

"That's like every employee in Walmart being a millionaire!" Zack said in astonishment.

"Yes. But the thing is, nobody on earth knows that each of the scientists work together. They all think that they are the single boss of their field. The Rebal fooled the government, they fooled humanity, they fooled the world," Reece said.

"And now the world will pay," I heaved.

"The Rebal was created ever since Blade came to power. At first, before the cure was found. Before the scientists became successful in their fields, they were zero. But now they're heroes. Or, should I say, a monster," Reece grumbled.

"Do you like the Tripartite?" Zack asked Reece.

"No," he replied darkly.

"But they are trying to stop Blade, right?" I said.

"They are just like him. They only do it because they want power," Reece sneered.

"Why are they called the Tripartite?" Zack asked.

"In Roman times, they had an executive branch called the tripartite. It was where there were three consuls, or presidents, if you will, who led the executive branch. *Tripartite* means 'three linked.' This is because there were three consuls," Morri explained.

"Very good," Reece remarked.

"How do you know that?" I asked Morri.

"Human computer, remember?" she said.

"Oh, yeah," I replied.

"That still doesn't explain why they are called that," Zack pushed.

"They are called this because there are three groups in the Tripartite," Reece started. "The Uprising, in Canada, the Rebellion, in South America, and the Alliance, in North America," Reece explained.

"That I did not know," Morri said.

"They are all linked and all allies. For the time being, at least," Reece added.

"When will the battle start?" I asked.

"Very soon, I fear. They are refusing to give their profits to Blade, and Blade's own money is going under. And so is the loyalty of his own men. They see what's happening, and they fear that Blade is on the losing side. And if Blade doesn't do something fast, his money will be gone. Leading to total and inevitable destruction. His only option is to take the money by force, but since Parkins controls trade, it's going to be tricky. Even I can't say who will win. But the tables are starting to turn. One scientist can fight against another, but one can't fight against eleven. This seems to be the problem Blade is in, and it's not a very easy one to clean up. And the fact that his enemies are across the ocean only adds to the problem. Blade never realized how much he depended on his fellow scientists' profit until now, but by now, it's too late. It looks like the Tripartite has victory on their side. But if they win, I can't say if it's for better or for worse." Reece breathed out heavily.

I looked down at my feet. This was all so much to take in. If the Tripartite was against us, then we'd have another problem to face. And if there was one thing I knew, it was that Blade was enough to deal with already.

"You know, you guys could be what they've been waiting for, a turning point in the battle. They know that Blade has children with powers like you, and they are afraid that he'll use them against them. You guys could be their key to success if you joined their side," Reece said.

"I doubt Blade will put his secret weapon at risk," Zack replied.

"I agree. If he risks using the children in the civil war, then by the end of the battle, there would surely be children that died, then his hand would be weakened. He wouldn't be able to take over the world," Morri added.

They were right. Even if Blade did win, he'd be vulnerable.

"Even worse," Reece started. "The Rebal have hidden themselves from the world for some time now. But they won't be able to hide the war. By the end of the battle, the world will know who they are and possibly even their aims. This could be the rise of the Rebal, or more likely the fall." He sighed.

We drove in silence for another fifteen minutes when I said, "How did you escape and be able to avoid Blade for so long?"

"Blade would've never expected me to turn. I was part of his personal guard, but then one day, while he walked out of his office, out of curiosity I looked into his files. That's where I learned his plans, that's when I knew he was mad. He wanted to create a new species on the planet, a species of human with special abilities. And he would be their ruler. But I also realized that to create a new species, he would have to make another species extinct, humans. I knew he would turn against his own soldiers, his own friends, to fulfill his delusions. He would have to kill every human on earth to execute his plans, even me. That's why I told other guards about his plans. And when I was sent to do my nightly guard duties, me and ten other vans of escapers drove off to Geneva. One of the vans didn't make it. That was the one with Morri in it," he said.

"She told us you couldn't even get her out of her cell," I said.

"It's best you don't push her about it. It's not something she likes to talk about," Reece replied.

I looked around the seat at Morri. She was asleep, so was Zack. Me and Reece were the only ones awake. I looked out the window into the night sky, the stars twinkling brightly, as if telling me not to give up. That there was still hope.

I looked back toward Geneva. Now it was only a string of lights in the distance. Hopefully we'd be far enough away that Blade wouldn't be able to find us, but like the stars read, all I could do was hope.

Suddenly, a beeping sound filled the van.

Reece screeched the van to a stop and yelled. "Hurry! It's a tracking device!"

Ava groaned and opened her eyes, lifting her head off my shoulder.

"What's going on?" she whispered to me, half asleep.

I shot out of my seat and patted myself down, nothing.

I grabbed Ava's arms, feeling for anything. When I didn't find anything, I crouched down to her legs.

"What are you doing!" Ava yelled.

"Someone's got a tracking device on them!" I yelled, setting her legs down.

"The Rebal have already homed into where we are!" Zack yelled over the panic in the back of the van.

"This is dangerously close to my headquarters!" Reece said. "We need to disable it immediately!" he roared.

"Nothing up here!" I said.

"Nothing in the back either!" Zack yelled.

Then who has it? I thought.

Suddenly I realized, Morri.

Reece probably caught on to me at the same time because he grabbed Morri by the shoulders turned her back to him. Sure enough, a red light was glowing through her shirt. He lifted up her shirt and blanched.

"It's implanted," he whispered.

The mood turned dead serious.

All of a sudden, the beeping noise increased. I looked down on my chest. A red light was glowing through my shirt as well.

I turned toward Ava. A red light was showing through her jeans as well.

She looked up at me, her face pale. I slowly turned to the back of the van. A light was glowing on every one of us. The Rebal were coming, and there was nothing we could do about it.

Part Four

Chapter 18

Tracked
Ava Jones

Ava glanced at Noah in horror, hoping this was some kind of terrible prank. If it was, she would knock him silly.

But judging by the look on his face, she knew this was no joke. This was a matter of life and death.

"W-what are we gonna do?" Ava stammered.

Reece slipped a knife out of his pocket, the shiny steel glinting in the moonlight.

"What we always do in these kinds of situations," Reece said sternly.

"What are you gonna do with the knife?" Jane shouted a little too fast.

The reality suddenly hit me. They'd have to cut the devices out. There was no other way.

Ava started to whimper. Noah took her hand and said, "We have to do this, guys. If we don't, we will risk falling into Blade's hands, or worse."

It wasn't a yes-or-no decision. All of them knew that.

Zack was the first to stand up. "Noah's right. I know Blade well enough that he won't want to deal with us anymore. He'll get rid of us. Permanently." Zack's voice nearly echoed off the van's walls.

Jayce looked down, avoiding everyone's gaze. Jane started to cry. Noah helped Ava up. They all got out of the car, Reece guiding us into a field.

When they got far enough from the van to meet Reece's needs, he turned on a flashlight. The light drowned out the glowing from our tracking devices almost completely.

He looked over everyone, almost as if waiting for a volunteer.

"How big are the devices?" Noah suddenly asked.

"Around the size of your fingernail," Morri said.

We all turned to her in annoyance.

"Morri! This is no time to tell jokes!" Jayce yelled at her.

"No, I'm serious. I remember the doctor putting the device in me," she explained.

"Why didn't you tell us about the tracking devices earlier!" Ava shouted at her.

"Like you, I was too caught up in escaping! Getting captured wasn't really on my mind then!" Morri shot back at Ava.

"Hush! Everyone!" Reece boomed. "I know this may be scary, but arguing won't change anything!"

"Quiet!" Noah roared.

The only sound alive at the time being now was the sudden and chilly gust of wind. Noah eyed all of them, glaring at everyone, even Ava.

"If you hadn't been wasting your time arguing, then you would've heard what I said!" he yelled. Even Reece looked to the ground in shame.

"You don't want to get the device cut out of you, right?" Noah started. They all shook their heads in agreement.

"Well, Morri gave us the answer," he said, more softly this time.

"What do you mean?" Morri asked.

"You said the tracking devices were only the size of a fingernail, right?" Noah asked Morri.

"Uh, yeah?" Morri replied, confused.

"Then I have a plan that can buy us all a good amount of time," Noah replied.

"Go ahead," Reece said, a grin crossing his face as he put his knife away.

"First, I'm gonna need a volunteer," Noah said.

Everybody looked around unsteadily.

"I will," Ava said, breaking the silence.

Morri rolled her eyes.

"This won't hurt, Ava," Noah said. He suddenly grinned. "At least I think it won't."

Ava stopped walking forward. "What do you mean?" Ava asked, cringing away.

"What I mean is that I don't even know if this will work or if it will hurt," he explained.

"Why are you smiling?" Ava asked.

"Because if it works, Blade will explode like a volcano," he said, smiling even bigger this time.

Ava smiled back at him. "I'm all in!" she said, excited.

The field suddenly erupted in noise.

"Count me in!" Jayce yelled.

"I don't care if it hurts. I want Blade to be hurt!" Zack whooped.

"Uh, I guess so," Jane said quietly.

"Whatever you say, boss," Morri agreed.

"Then it's settled," Reece said, putting his hands in the air. "We'll see if Noah's plan works, and if not…" he suddenly stopped himself, the field quieting down.

"I have only one request before we start, though," Reece started.

"What?" Noah asked.

"Keep it down."

Chapter 19

Back on Track
Ava Jones

Ava slowly extended her leg out to Noah, preparing for the worst to come. He almost had his hand over her leg where the tracking device was when he suddenly spoke up. "This tracking device's sound waves report back to the control tower in Rebal International where we are, right?" he asked Morri.

"Yeah, pretty much all tracking devices, GPS, and checkpoints report back through sound," she explained.

"Good," he said, reaching back down to Ava's leg. She squeezed her eyes shut, half expecting the Rebal to show up right then, when suddenly the beeping stopped.

"What did you do?" she asked, looking down at her leg. He took his hand off, and the glow was gone.

"I muted the tracking device. They can't pick up where you are now," he explained.

He put his hand on her back and helped her up.

"I didn't feel a thing," she said, astonished.

"Brilliant, just brilliant!" Reece commented.

Ava turned toward him and smiled. "Thanks, Noah," she said.

We suddenly locked eyes, his gaze stuck on hers.

"Uh, can I go next?" Jayce spoke up, breaking the silence.

Ava looked around. Everyone was staring at them. She started to blush rapidly.

"We'll talk later," Noah said, bringing her back to reality.

"Uh, right, later," she said, looking down.

Noah turned to Jayce and started back up on getting rid of the tracking devices.

She ran to the van, shutting the door behind her.

How could I have been so stupid! she thought. *Trying to get close to him with everyone around me! He probably thinks I'm a freak!* she realized. Then she remembered what he said, that being different wasn't easy. He'd lived his life thinking he was a freak too. When they had that conversation back at school, it felt so good to know that she wasn't the only alien in the world. Even better, it was he who had a power too. She'd always had a secret crush on him in third grade, all the way up to now. She used to worry that someone would figure out, that she'd be made fun of. But now she wished that that was what she had to worry about. It didn't matter anymore. School, friends, popularity. That was all a distant past. Now someone was trying to hunt her down and kill her, she was in the middle of nowhere, and on top of that, her parents were gone. Everything was a big mess. Even though she was here with Noah, that she knew he would protect her, she missed her friends, her family, even her dumb volleyball tryouts that she dreaded. A tear slid down her cheek. This wasn't the first time she'd had a breakdown. In the cell, she had at least five. She never thought she'd leave, never thought she'd live to see the sun the next day. Even Jane and the others didn't help her at all. All she wanted was something, someone familiar to see. And that's when Noah came. He got them out, freed them, beat Blade. He'd done everything a good leader should do. He was more than a leader, he was a hero. But even she knew that Blade had a whole army of powers. They'd be after them, there was no doubt about it. She knew that not even Noah could beat Blade. He needed us. The only question she had, the only answer she wanted to know, was what Blade was up to. He'd stolen or even killed her parents, he'd stolen Noah's family, he'd broken Noah, he had them on the run for their lives. What more did he want. And why did he want it?

Jane opened the door and sat down next to her on the seat, close enough that their shoulders were touching.

"Things didn't go so well with Noah, huh?" she said.

She sniffled. "It's not that. I just miss everything, everybody that I used to know," she replied.

"That's what Blade wants. He wants you to miss what used to be. He wants you to want what you used to be. Then he gets you to do things to get that back, tells you, 'Jane, you'll see your family again, just kill one more person.'" She sighed.

"Kill one more person?" Ava yelled.

"Blade wants you to be prepared to face the world, wants you to get used to killing. I saw friends that I thought loved and cared for me turn into savages, bloodthirsty killers. Zack and I were some of the few who resisted him," she explained.

"What do you mean face the world?" Ava asked.

"Blade has a dream, a delusion to destroy humanity so he can build a new species, us, the powers. He tells us and likes to think of it as a cleansing of the world," she said in disgust.

"He's psycho! He can't destroy the human race! He's a human, for crying out loud!" Ava fumed.

"He believes that once he takes over the world, his children will still be loyal to him, and that he'll be their king. And if he's the king over them, he's the king of the world," she explained.

"He's nuts! All he wants is power! He's like a shark that eats to much chum!" Ava yelled.

Jane started to laugh. "That's a pretty good description." She chuckled.

She didn't feel like laughing. What Jane had just told her made her want to get rid of Blade all the more.

"Do you miss your family?" Ava asked, now sad again.

Jane started to stare into space. "There's a good chance they're already dead…" she started.

"Don't say that! You have to stay faithful. You have to remember them," she said sternly.

Jane's eyes started to well up. "Thinking about them only makes the pain worse." She cried.

Ava suddenly was embarrassed at her outburst. She didn't know what she'd been through. Ava couldn't judge her about anything.

"I'm sorry, it's just that I can't give up on my family. I know we can rescue them," she said.

"It's fine," Jane said, wiping her eyes. "Sometimes you just have to remember the good things about your family, right?" she asked.

"Right," Ava said, trailing off.

"About you and Noah, it's fine if you like him. I'm not gonna get in the way of you guys," she said.

"It's not you I'm worried about," Ava started.

"Oh, Morri. Don't worry. I'll make sure she stays out of it too," she said.

"It's not her either. It's him, it's Noah I'm worried about. He's just changed so much. He used to be that handsome boy at the old high school we were at, and now…"

"I understand. The same thing happened to Zack when we used to live in Havana. He'd been my boyfriend since sixth grade, and when the Rebal took us, he grew so protective over me, he turned into a man," she said.

"How'd you guys hook up then?" Ava asked.

"I guess destiny has its ways," she said, yawning

Ava stared at Noah, the flashlight beam illuminating his stern face. He didn't turn his attention to anything but the well-being of the group. He was so protective, like Jane had described Zack.

Ava only wished destiny would turn to their favor, like Jane and Zack's did.

Jane started to scoot away from her then said, "You want some advice on boys?"

"Really anything could come in handy right about now," she said.

"Don't like Noah for what you think he is. Like him for who he thinks he is." She climbed into the back seat and buckled up. Everyone else poured into the van after her.

"We got everyone rid of the tracking devices," Noah said as he sat down next to Ava and buckled up.

"That's good," she said.

"About saying that I could talk to you later, it looks like we're going to be planning and figuring out info about my family and the Rebal when we get to Reece's hideout. We probably won't have time to talk," he said.

Ava turned away from him and looked out the window at the swaying and endless lines of grass in the Switz meadows. The starry night cast an eerie glow over the endless fields.

She only had one question about Jane's advice, who did Noah think he was?

Chapter 20

Change of Plans
Blade Mercantile

Blade looked over the holographic map that covered the whole left wall of his office. He stared intently at North America, South America, and Canada on the map. Today was an odd day. For three months Dr. Parkins and the other scientists had been overseas because of a so-called project that would gain the Rebal organization more profit. But that didn't explain why they had brought half of the Rebal army over there. At first he had assumed that they had brought guards over to protect their faculties, but so far, no more faculties had been made, he hadn't heard anything whatsoever of the project or its success, and worst of all, the money that Blade needed to keep the organization up and running hadn't been sent for two months. Something wasn't right. Blade sensed it from the start. His own guards were on the verge of breaking their own loyalty, and he barely was able to keep supplying his powers in training the equipment they needed to start the takeover. He was about to fly over to Dr. Parkins himself and knock some sense into him. He couldn't keep playing Mr. Nice Guy. Dire and desperate measures would soon need to be taken in order to keep the organization from going under, even if it meant taking resources by force. And as of today, instead of supply ships lining the American and Canadian coast to bring him supplies, battleships and troop transports took their place. Were they under attack, or more likely, would they be preparing to attack? He sensed that a conflict would arise, and soon.

He suddenly heard a knock at the door. He quickly turned off the holographic map and strutted to the door, fixing his hair and putting the nicest face he could muster on him.

"Who is it?" he said through the microphone.

"Agent Brock, sir," the voice replied.

"Very well, come in," Blade said.

The huge oak door slowly opened, and Blade had to step back so it wouldn't hit him. He straightened his gold tie as the agent stepped in.

"Do you have any updates on the escape of the powers in the third section cells?" Blade ordered.

"We must have a discussion over that," the agent explained.

"Very well," Blade replied.

Blade walked to the head chair, letting his fingers trace over the gold plating that decorated the armrests.

"Have a seat, please," Blade ordered the agent.

He walked to the seat directly across from Blade, his dark glasses shining in the light of the crystal chandelier hanging above them.

"The progress on the breach?" Blade reminded the agent.

"Of course, sir. Sorry, sir. We have unfortunate news that they escaped our attempt to subdue them without harm, sir," the agent explained.

Blade rubbed his forehead in grief. Never before had so many powers escaped unscathed.

"Please remind me who escaped," Blade said in annoyance.

"Morri Thresh, who can store data in her mind like a computer. She is a level one, sir. Jane Mahoe, who can turn invisible. A number two, sir. Zack Gupta, who has super strength, and a number three, sir. Ava Jones, who can control gravitational pull, a level three, sir. Jayce Smith, who can run supersonic speeds, a level two, sir. And finally, Noah Tone, who can control sound waves, a level three, sir," the agent replied.

By the time it took the agent to get to the third escapee, Blade's hands were already trembling with anger.

He clenched his jaw and said slowly and threateningly, "Please repeat the last name, Agent."

"Uh, Noah Tone, sir?"

Blade exploded. "You useless mole rats!" he screeched. "How could you have let three level-three powers escape!" he roared.

The agent backed away in horror.

"For a reminder, there are only twelve level threes in existence! With three of them in one group, they could be completely unstoppable!" He boomed.

"Uh, then, I suppose it's good you never trained them then, sir?" the agent stammered.

"Never trained them!" Blade shrieked, nearly to the brink of ripping the agent's head off. "All you need to do is tell them what they're capable of! And by the looks of it, they know good and well how to get defenseless and powerless agents like you off their backs!" Blade screamed.

"What do you, uh, suggest we do then, sir?" the agent said, cringing back from him.

Blade put his head in his hands. How much more of this could he bear to hear?

"Locate their tracking devices and hunt them down," he growled.

"Uh, we also have unfortunate news about their tracking devices, sir," the agent started.

Blade gave the agent a death stare. "What happened now?" he yelled.

"We lost the tracking signal, sir," the agent said in defeat.

"You what!" Blade roared.

He reached across the desk and grabbed the agent by the collar.

"You go to where you lost their signal and look for them from there, and don't come back until you find them. Or else you will spend the rest of your miserable life guarding a facility in the never-ending winter of northern Russia, outside," he seethed threateningly.

The agent took the treat seriously. A cold sweat broke out around the rim of his glasses.

Blade let go of the agent and sat back down in his seat.

"Go. Now," he growled.

"We have another problem, sir," the agent replied in terror.

"Oh, I just can't wait to hear this one!" Blade yelled in annoyance.

"We believe the command tower's radar was affected by the attack of the youths. Their position in Geneva is unknown," the agent stammered.

"Isn't that unfortunate," Blade said pitifully. "And I expect that you will ask me for their coordinates now?" Blade said in annoyance.

"Uh, sir, yes, sir," the agent said, sitting a bit straighter in his seat.

"Whatever!" Blade said. He took out his laptop and searched for the last location of their coordinates. Once he found them, he downloaded them onto a GPS.

He handed the GPS to the agent, who took it quickly.

"Sir, thank you, sir," the agent replied, not even looking at him.

"Now remember, don't come back until you find them," Blade sneered. "Or else."

"Sir, I understand, sir!" the agent said in attention.

"Now go," Blade said, shooing him away.

The agent quickly left the room, not even shutting the door behind him.

Blade smiled to himself. *Perhaps the guards' loyalty hasn't gone afar!* he thought to himself.

He picked up the phone and dialed Dr. Parkins.

"Yes, Blade," Parkins said almost immediately.

"There has been a change of plans, Doctor. A security breach in the third section cells of Rebal International had three escapees who are level threes. We will turn all of our power, force, and attention into capturing these dangerous rebellers. This is a mistake that we will not ignore," Blade replied.

"Yes, Dr. Blade. I will inform my side of the Rebal of this. We will not disappoint you," Parkins said swiftly.

"And by the way, what do you have to say for yourself about the resources that I need that haven't come for three months?" Blade said, trying to hide his anger as best as he could.

"Don't worry, they will come very soon," Dr. Parkins reassured him. "And we are preparing to send a large amount of our Rebal forces to you. Be prepared to take them into your facilities," Dr. Parkins added.

Maybe I was wrong about them betraying me, Blade thought to himself.

"Very well, and send the resources soon," Blade reminded Parkins. He hung up and set his phone on the desk.

"Geneva, Geneva," he mumbled to himself. He suddenly smiled. "Reece. Perhaps we have two enemies on the line!" He smiled then turned back to the holographic map. He wouldn't let anyone beat him. After all, no one ever had. Well, almost no one.

CHAPTER 21

Betrayed Agent Brock

Agent Brock quickly stepped out of the Rebal International doors, never intending to go back. He couldn't believe he had succeeded. He was the mouse going into the lion's den. It was a miracle he ever got out.

He scurried to his black F-150, hopping into the front seat.

"Capturing the powers alone!" he scoffed. "Boy, would that be a nightmare!"

He stepped on the gas and sped in the opposite direction of where Tone and his comrades were.

He roughly took his phone out of his pocket with one hand, driving with the other.

"Mr. Parkins," he started. "I have acquired the powers' coordinates."

"Very good," Parkins replied. "You have done well, Agent."

"Sir, I do wish Dr. Blade was the least bit understanding as you, sir," Brock added.

"As do I!" Parkins laughed. "If he was, this war wouldn't be starting in the first place."

"I understand, sir," Brock replied.

"And I intend to finish this war. Swiftly," Parkins added.

"The team is waiting outside the Quick Trip, am I right?" Brock asked.

"Yes, prepared and loaded," Parkins reassured him. "When you meet the team, remind them not to hurt the youths. We want them in top condition."

"Understood, sir," Brock said.

"If you meet any Rebal resistance, we will come to your aid quickly," Parkins reminded Brock.

"Sir, I am almost completely confident that if we met the Rebal, we would knock their socks off," Brock replied.

"As am I," Parkins laughed. "As am I."

Brock slipped the phone into his pocket. One of the names of the escapees sounded familiar, that Noah Tone. Yes! He had been the boy he'd captured days before. His time with the Rebal had been short. Maybe they could make common ground together since they've met before. After all, knowing that Brock had betrayed the Rebal would make them the best of friends, he hoped.

CHAPTER 22

Danger Is Everywhere
Ava Jones

Ava was falling, falling down a hole that seemed to have no end. Was it hours, days, years that she'd been rocketing down the pitch-black pit? As she was falling, images, memories formed into existence around her.

Her mom helping her cook for the first time, her father with her at girls' camp, Ava at volleyball practice with her friends. It was the same in every image, laughter, joy, and happiness.

A tear slid down her cheek. She suddenly started to sob, remembering everything that she had once been, everything that was gone.

Her images darkened, and images of her and her friends locked in cells, the Rebal kidnapping her, guards, guns, blaring sirens, screams, Ava and her friends suffering, and her parents gone overtook the good memories.

She froze in terror, shaking with fear. This was what Ava was now. This was what was now her world.

Blade's face suddenly appeared, getting bigger and bigger, his evil laugh echoing off the unseen cavern walls. His face now overtook everything around her, his eyes turned red, and he opened his mouth. He swallowed her family, her friends, the things Ava treasured. All that was left now was all the bad memories, the world she was in now.

Blade's mouth inched toward her. She could literally smell his breath as his jaws clamped shut.

Ava shot up and gasped. She was still alive? Her clothes clung to her skin, the environment around her was cramped, and the air reeked of sweat. As her eyes adjusted, Ava saw that they were still in Reece's van. She was also clinging tightly to Noah. She inhaled sharply, embarrassed and glad that he was close to her. She heard Jayce's and Zack's snoring in the back of the van and sat up straighter.

Just a dream, she thought. *Just a dream.*

"Nightmare?" Noah asked.

"Bad one," Ava replied, remembering all the awful things she had seen.

Noah pulled her closer. She sank into his chest and sighed with relief. Around him she felt safe.

"Don't worry, Ava, everything will be all right. Once we beat the Rebal, everything will be back to normal," he reassured her.

"I want things to stay this way," she said sadly.

His eyes suddenly turned dark. "So does Blade."

They stayed like that for the rest of the ride, Noah holding her for comfort, him holding her to help her feel better. She knew Noah had feelings for her. Ava just didn't know how strong they were.

Suddenly the course of the van changed, sloping upward. They all fell back against their seats. Most people woke up from the disturbance.

Noah looked out the window and released his hold on her. The van lurched to a stop.

He unbuckled. "We are here now," he said, almost disappointed.

Ava sat up straight and looked out the window. In front of her stood a large ranch house. The lights were on too. This was not what she had expected to be a hideout. She half expected a trench to be here.

Reece opened the garage doors, the wooden doors slowly sliding upward. What now stood in its place was a large metal wall.

"Dude, can't we just park out here?" Jayce asked.

"Watch and be amazed," Reece said, grinning.

He opened a secret keypad on the ceiling of the van and punched in something. The keypad shut quickly, and the ground under them started to rumble and shake. Suddenly, a grinding sound filled the air. She looked at the metal wall, and suddenly it split into four parts, each part sliding away, revealing a dark corridor in its place.

"I totally need one of these at my house!" Jayce laughed.

Noah quickly buckled back up. None of them knew what was in store for them, and Ava had to admit that after everything they've been through, it was better to be safe than sorry.

Reece kicked up the engine, hit the gas, and they started cruising into the darkness. Every few feet, a light switched on as they passed it. The van came to a halt, and they started to spin in a circle. Ava and Noah looked out the window, and the faint glow of the lights revealed a metal turntable underneath them. The spinning stopped, and they heard something lock into place.

Once again, Reece clicked open the secret keypad and punched in numbers.

Bing! A green light lit up next to them, and their elevation suddenly dropped. Ava looked out under the van and saw that the metal turntable was gone and they were descending down a slope.

They were in total darkness for about thirty seconds. The looks of uncertainty and fear were plastered on the gang's faces, dimly illuminated by the poor lighting.

The dark was then replaced with a slow but gradual ray of light. Ava looked out the windshield and saw a small speck of light. Little by little, the speck grew and grew as they raced closer until they drove through the tunnel and were bathed by bright, blinding light. As Ava's eyes adjusted, she was struck with amazement. If she thought that the house was big before, she hadn't seen the inside.

It was a factory. To her right stood a huge screen showing a map of Switzerland, red dots marking each Rebal compound, and a surprisingly large amount of blue dots surrounding each compound, Tripartite strongholds!

Computers and racks of suits lined the wall and an impressive assortment of weapons hung along the top of the wall, everything reaching to nearly fifty feet in the air. Metal ramps lined the walls everywhere, ensuring a quick and accessible path to whatever supplies anyone needed.

The wall to her right had her even more astonished. A huge tank with a terrorizing assortment of missiles, guns, and armor stood before her. Above it in midair was a helicopter with two gigantic machine gun barrels on each side, missiles lined the wings, looking big enough to completely obliterate anything. Both the tank and the copter were gray, with a symbol of a yellow triangle with three yellow dots on the corners of the triangle. The symbol was encased in a black circle.

The symbol of the Tripartite! Three linked! Ava thought.

But what surprised her even more was that there were people bustling around the immense garage.

Reece must've sensed their awe and quickly spoke up. "What stands before you is my headquarters. The people you see here are my fellow comrades that escaped Rebal International with me, and a few are also a part of the Tripartite Organization."

"Wait, I thought you disliked the Tripartite," Morri asked.

Everyone quickly turned toward him, eyeing him suspiciously.

"When we were on the run, we didn't know where to go. When the Tripartite got word of our little escape, they offered me a place to hide out, they offered me protection. There was no way I could pass that up," Reece sighed.

"I understand," Noah said.

"So this is your garage, huh," Jayce said in amazement.

"It would appear so," Reece replied.

"Not too shabby," Zack commented.

"They gave you a tank and a helicopter?" Ava asked in disbelief.

"Not at first, of course, but every once in a while they hire me and a group of my elite soldiers to carry out top secret missions for the Tripartite. They sent me these as gifts," He explained.

"I wish I got stuff like this for my birthday!" Jayce whined.

They all laughed. Reece gave them a tour, showing them around the garage and introducing them to some of the people who worked in the garage.

He showed them around the tank and copter, but since she was afraid of heights, Ava refused to go into the copter's cockpit.

When they finally got to the main screen showing the map of Switzerland, Reece turned around and stopped.

"Before I tell you about this, I have to tell you something important. The people here are not a part of the Tripartite organization," he told us.

"But I thought you were hired to go on top secret missions," Jane replied.

"*Top secret* are the key words. We are not allowed to tell anybody anything about the missions we carry out or execute," Reece said seriously.

"Ouch," Jayce said.

"You guys may not have information kept away from you, though. You guys are…special," Reece added.

Jayce pumped a fist in the air. "Yeah! Does that mean you can tell us about your missions?" Jayce asked.

"Don't get ahead of yourself, boy," Reece chuckled.

"Bummer," Jayce said in defeat. Zack rolled his eyes.

"So what's this map all about then?" Ava asked curiously.

"As I was saying, since we are not a part of the Tripartite, we are something different," Reece started.

"Like what?" Noah asked.

"We call ourselves the Switz Resistance, SWR for short. Since we did not want anything to do with the Tripartite, the Tripartite gave us Switzerland to establish our own compounds and strongholds as we wished. Since Switzerland is small, we have easily fortified the entire country. It is nearly completely under our control," Reece said proudly.

"Why don't the Rebal kick you guys out?" Zack asked.

"As I told you in the van, Blade still thinks that the other scientists are on his side, and since the Tripartite supplies the SWR, Blade thinks that we are Rebal as well," Reece replied.

"So that's why you've stayed hidden for so long!" Ava exclaimed enthusiastically.

"Indeed it is, and fortunately for us, if the Rebal forces in Switzerland figure out about our aim to destroy the Rebal and attack, we will have a sufficient amount of forces to hold them back for some time, enough time for reinforcements from the Tripartite to arrive," Reece added.

"But it looks like you guys completely outnumber the Rebal," Noah said, gesturing to the countless number of blue dots on the screen.

"We may have power, but the Rebal have numbers. Every one of their compounds is heavily guarded by around one thousand fully equipped guards, whereas each one of our strongholds only houses around fifty soldiers, each elite and highly trained. It would take one hundred of our strongholds to take just one of the Rebal compounds," Reece said darkly.

Looking at the map, Ava saw what he meant. Since there were around four Rebal compounds, plus Rebal's capitol, Rebal International, she estimated that there were roughly around six thousand Rebal guards, and that was only in Switzerland. If what Reece had said was right, how much power was in the UK, Russia, China, the Middle East, Africa, Indonesia, and Australia? The Rebal owned all of them, and there were still more to be named.

On the other hand, the SWR had around three hundred small blue dots surrounding the border, each of the Rebal compounds, and many others were in completely unpopulated places, such as the SWR headquarters they were in right now.

"So this is your best stronghold?" Morri said.

"Yes, it is," Reece replied. "We have an extra fifty soldiers in headquarters for your protection," Reece added. "Most other strongholds have only a jeep and armored car to protect them, but we have taken special care to surround each stronghold with secret machine gun nests. You'd be surprised how much they slow the enemy down," Reece laughed, a sly grin across his face.

"Rebal International has five jets, and plus, they also have around twenty tanks, one hundred armored cars, and around five hundred jeeps," Zack said in defeat. "How do you expect to defeat them?" Zack asked.

"We never planned to defeat them, let alone bring them at mercy. All we're here for is to buy the Tripartite time to prepare. We're the front line of defense," Reece said, almost proud.

"Being in the front lines is like, I don't know, a death sentence!" Jayce put in.

"As ironic as it may sound," Reece started, turning off the map and replacing it with a radar. "We should be, in fact, the last of the Tripartite teams to have our cover blown. Each of our soldiers are highly trained as spies, master gunmen, and in stratagem. We keep a very low profile, and the Rebal barely notice us. We have the best equipment, soldiers, and strongholds. We are expected to be the first to react to the start of the war or to start a war ourselves. As we are the team that resides in the Rebal's home country, there is an extremely high chance that the war will start right here."

"Whoa," Ava said. "Should we get out then?" she asked.

"It's too risky. There are probably Rebal crawling everywhere right now due to your escape. You will have to stay here until it's safe," Reece insisted.

Everyone cast one another nervous glances. Was this the end of our journey or the beginning? Would the war start and they would be right in the middle of it?

"You should get settled while you have the chance. We don't know how long you will be here," Reece said, walking down the ramp.

Everyone followed him, gloomy and defeated looks on their faces. This was a dangerous place to be. They all knew it. But was it like they had a choice? Ava would take her chances here rather than risk being recaptured by the Rebal. She knew everyone else did too.

Reece stopped at a large metal door. He took a card out of his pocket and swiped it on a keypad built into the door. A green light appeared on the keypad, and the door slid down.

A dimly lit hallway stood in front of them. The walls were, of course, metal. Reece was not kidding. They took security seriously down here. He seemed even more paranoid than her at the time, maybe even more paranoid than her mom back at home. The thought made Ava ache. It reminded her how much she missed everything.

Remember what Noah said, Ava thought. *Once everything's over, it will all be back to normal.* But would it?

Part Five

CHAPTER 23

Rescued or Trapped
Zack Gupta

Zack's new bedroom was like heaven compared to the cell back at Rebal International. It took all the will he could muster not to collapse on the bed and dream forever, to never wake back up into this horrible nightmare. Jane, at least, brightened everything up around him. Ever since they met in Havana in sixth grade, his life had been better, but when the Rebal captured them, Zack knew it had been partially his fault. He had dragged her into this, after all. He was the one who asked her out. Jane always said that he blamed himself too much, but Zack wasn't so sure. After he'd refused to do Blade's twisted training methods, he convinced Jane to do the same and should've known Blade would lock them up. It was his fault they had been through all this. Should he have killed just one person to meet Blade's standards so he and Jane wouldn't be in constant danger? Should he have risked his and Jane's life when he refused to listen to Blade? He pushed the thoughts quickly out of his mind. He still remembered Ian, Aubrey, and Josh greedily killing innocent human beings during training. It wasn't fair. It wasn't right.

He still remembered all those countless days in the cell, him and Jane separated. Seeing her suffer, it was the worst and saddest time he'd been through. But it also fueled his anger toward Blade. In no time at all, it was clear that he was the only number three power in the cells. He was the leader, no objections about it. Zack had to admit that he was in fact a bit jealous when Noah took over his role, but he was a good guy and led the team well. After all, without him, they would've never escaped that horrible prison.

Even though he wouldn't dare admit it to Jane, the thing he missed most in the cell was Havana, Cuba. The cobblestone roads, the trading markets along the plaza streets, the countless palm and banana trees lining every curb, the never-ending sea stretching out before him, the sand digging between his toes as the waves lapped at his jeans. That was what he missed most, home. He didn't know his mami or papa too much. They had always been busy with work, his Mami a travel agent and his father usually at some other girlfriend's house. He never told Mami about it, though. He tended to the house himself. All throughout fifth grade life was steady, every day brought the same thing, then he met Jane. Jane gave him a purpose in life, a reason to live, the moment he saw her, and he told her this a thousand times. She melted his feet to his sandals. She always just blushed and looked away when he told her that. But she was, in fact, beautiful. When he asked her out the first time, she just ran away. But since he was stubborn, he didn't give up. The second time he asked, she said that she didn't have time, even though he could tell she liked him. She just wouldn't admit it. By now he knew she was shy, so the third time he waited until everyone was gone and asked if she wanted to help him gather bananas with him. She accepted since people did this all the time, and there was nothing particularly romantic about it. He took her to the beach and showed her the highest banana tree, doubting she could get halfway up. He only wanted her to give up and he would do it for her and become somewhat her hero. But she climbed to the top all right and threw the gigantic banana bunch right on his forehead, and the bananas slammed into him, the gooey substance dripping onto his shirt. She came down with a fuss, cleaning his shirt in the ocean and apologizing countless times before she finally asked, "How did you not fall over?"

Hiding his secret for so long, he decided that if this would be his girlfriend, it would be okay to tell her about his power.

Telling her about his power should've sent her running for home, but miraculously, she seemed anything but surprised about it.

"I sensed something different, something powerful in your *espiritu*," which is Cuban for "spirit."

Zack asked her how, and she told him that her family carried an ancient heritage all the way back when Cubans were a native people, and that her ancestors were leaders in ancient rituals and that it's passed down throughout the generations. She called it her gift.

They sat there in silence for a moment, and she told him that before they go on their first date, she needed to tell Zack something. She told him about her power. He'd never felt so happy, so free in his life, and from then on him and Jane decided to stick together forever.

Then of course the Rebal had to come and ruin everything. End of story for them. At least it seemed like that until Noah came along. Now they were criminals, outlaws on the run. And they had nowhere to go, except in an SWR stronghold. Where a war was about to break out. Where Blade would be.

"Uh, sir. Your room?" the soldier asked, waving his hand at the entrance.

"Of course, sorry. It's amazing," Zack said as he stepped inside.

"Enjoy," the soldier said and walked away.

Zack had just collapsed onto the bed, his train of thought still fresh in his mind, when the door swung open.

"Zack!" Jane said as she scurried toward the bed.

"What is it?" Zack asked.

"Noah called a team meeting!" Jane said happily. She always acted like this in serious situations. She felt like she was doing something important.

He groaned and sat up on the bed, rubbing his temples.

"Maybe next time he should call a team nap," Zack grumbled.

"Zack! This is serious! All of us have a huge part in this," Jane pushed.

"This just keeps getting better!" he moaned. "We almost get killed escaping prison, we travel twenty miles to hide out in a city, then we meet some guy who traps us in the middle of a war! And now we're going to plan an attack that will undoubtedly bring the Rebal to its downfall. Great," Zack said in annoyance.

Jane had a hurt look on her face.

"I thought we were supposed to help the team," she said quietly.

"We did," he said. "How much more will we need to help?" he added.

"I didn't," Jane retorted.

"Yes, you did! You…helped a lot," Zack pushed out.

"You don't even know what I did," Jane sniffled.

He sat down next to her on the bed. "Jane, you saved me."

"How?" she said angrily.

"All those days in the cell, seeing you was what kept me alive. It gave me a reason not to die. I knew I couldn't give up on you. You were my lifeline. And I was yours," he said sternly.

She looked up at him, still doubt on her face, but also sympathy.

"All that matters now is that we're safe," Jane said. "And out of that horrible place."

"I'm sorry for getting us there," Zack said sadly.

She grabbed his head and turned it so he was facing her.

"That was not your fault," she insisted.

Zack looked her in the eye.

"Then whose was it?"

"Blade's," Jane said sourly. "Just saying his name makes me want to—"

Zack stopped her with a kiss. She was surprised at first, but then wrapped her arms around his waist.

They broke away, and Zack held her in his arms.

"Our days with Blade are over," he said after a while. "We're going back to Havana, no matter what stands in our way."

"But what about the others?" she said quietly.

"They don't know what they're up against. I'll do my best to convince them to go back home and forget everything like us. It is their choice," Zack said.

"Zack, we can't leave them," Jane ordered.

"But they can leave us," he said.

Jane looked down at the ground. She knew he was right about them not being able to beat Blade. They'd seen how powerful he was.

"What if their plan isn't about Blade?" Jane asked.

"Then we'll go along with them, but there has to be nothing about Blade involved," he replied. "Then it's straight to Havana," Zack added.

She nodded, and he set her on the ground.

"Let's go," Zack said.

CHAPTER 24

Unexpected Visitor
Noah Tone

I watched as Zack and Jane entered the room. When they sat down, I looked over everyone. The whole team was here and ready to fight. I was impressed and grateful for their support.

"Before we start, Noah, we need a name," Jayce spoke up, ending the silence.

"Puhleeze," Morri said in annoyance.

"You would think he'd come up with a crazy one already," Zack smirked.

"I did!" Jayce shot back. "We'll be called...the Universe Champions!" He beamed.

I looked at him in disbelief.

"What! It's pretty cool, right?" Jayce added.

"Moving on," I said. "Ava, do you have any ideas?" I asked.

Everyone looked at her and waited for her response. She started to blush under all the pressure. "Who? Me?" she asked.

"Who else would your boyfriend be talking about?" Morri snickered.

I cast an angry glance at Morri, and she sank back into her seat.

I looked at Ava. "It's fine. We'll ask someone else."

"No!" she yelled.

Everyone at the table cast her angry and annoyed glances. She looked down at her feet. "I, I have an idea," she said, embarrassed.

"What is it already! I'm dying to figure out what our name will be," Jayce whined.

"The First Strike," she said plainly.

"Why?" Jane asked.

"It makes sense. We're the first people I know that has ever stood up to Blade in his own territory," Morri explained.

"What should we call the members?" I asked Ava.

"Strikes."

The team and I nodded our heads in approval.

"First Strike," I repeated. "The Strikers."

The name was perfect, even though it might have come from an insignificant rebellion force like us.

Jayce was beaming. "Awesome!" he shouted. "I'm part of the First Strike! I'm a superhero!" he yelled.

"Not yet you aren't. You need to do something heroic," Morri said.

"I sped us all out of Rebal International!" Jayce retorted.

"Good point," I said. "I guess that means all of us are superheroes," I added.

Jane looked sad for some reason.

"So, boss, what's the plan?" Ava put in.

I looked at her and smiled.

"We're gonna rescue my family," I said strongly.

Zack looked like he would explode.

"Is something wrong?" I asked.

"You mean no Blade?" Jane said happily.

"No Blade," I reassured her.

Zack cleared his throat. "So what are we going to do then?" he pushed out.

"We're gonna need someone smart. We're gonna need the internet," I said.

"Morri?" Ava asked.

Morri straightened in her seat and stood at attention.

"What do you want me to do?" Morri asked.

"Is there a website that gives you information about the Rebal?" I asked.

"Yeah, it's called Reb.com."

"Then that's where we're going," I said quickly. "Morri is going to figure out the location of my family members, and we are going to find them. Any questions?" I asked.

I should've known that Jayce would raise his hand.

"Yes?" I said impatiently.

"What are the rest of us gonna do?" Jayce said curiously.

"Your parts will come after we figure out the location of my family members," I explained, looking over the table. The serious and worthy faces of my comrades filled me with joy. "Morri will be with me while we try to figure out the locations. The rest of you guys can get some sleep in. You're going to need it. This will probably take us a while anyway," I explained.

"I'll stay with you, Noah," Ava added.

Morri rolled her eyes.

"Are you sure you don't want some rest?" I asked her.

"No, I'm fine. I want to help you in this," she explained.

"It's settled then," Zack said, gripping the side of the table. His tone was disappointed for some reason.

Jane led Zack out of the room, while Jayce scurried back down to the garage, obviously wanting to get inside the tank or helicopter.

That left me, Morri, and Ava. The mission had started.

"We need a computer, right?" Morri said, breaking the silence.

"Do they have one?" Ava asked.

"What do you think, genius? They had a computer that takes up half the garage!" Morri yelled.

"I was talking about a computer that we could carry!" Ava shouted.

"Come on, guys! Break it up!" I said, standing between both of them. "How do you expect us to get anywhere acting like this?"

"Sorry," Ava said.

"Suck-up," Morri sneered.

Ava shot her a glare.

"Let's just get going," I interjected.

Morri quickly hurried into her room.

"Where is she going?" I asked Ava.

"Who knows," Ava said wryly.

We just sat out there for a while until Morri returned with a computer. Reece followed behind her.

"Why is he here?" I asked.

"Reece has been on the site before. He can help us get to your family," Morri explained.

Me and Ava exchanged nervous glances.

"You told him about our plan?" Ava said.

"Why not?" Morri asked.

"You can trust me," Reece said, sitting down. "The same thing happened to my family, and now they're gone. I don't want you to go through the same thing I did."

"Okay," I said. "But if we do find out where my family is, then were going to get John first. He's only three," I explained.

"They took a three-year-old?" Reece asked as if it was a good thing.

"Yeah, but we don't know where they took him," I said.

"They're getting more desperate. That's a good sign," Reece replied.

It wasn't such a good thing to me.

"Anyway," Ava said. "We need you and Morri to figure out their locations."

"Very well. If you think that you need any help on your mission, I'll send soldiers to assist you. The difficulty of the mission always depends on the compound's security," Reece added.

"We'll see to it if we need to," I replied.

Morri flipped open the laptop. About three minutes later, she spoke up. "Okay, Reece. I'm on it."

Reece slid over next to her and started scrolling through something, then he clicked a link. The Rebal website was more like a job recruitment page, not an enlistment into the army.

"Why does it say that all the Rebal do is run private businesses?" I asked.

"I guess that's what all the scientists do," Ava said.

I thought back to what Reece said about the scientists. But I didn't understand why they had so many soldiers if they needed to be running private businesses.

"Ava is very well right. When normal citizens sign up to work for the Rebal, they think that they will be helping to gather and ship supplies or work in an office, but the Rebal turn them into soldiers to guard the money and resources instead. They turn them into their army even though they don't know it. Many just assume they take great precaution in protecting their profit and resources. Very few are picked out to actually supply the resources. The Rebal only take the smartest recruits to do that job," Reece explained.

"Do those people turn into scientists?" I asked Reece, remembering all the nurses and doctors I saw at Rebal International.

"They do. The rank of Rebal is determined whether you are a scientist or not. The guards answer to the facility or compound police and clerks, the police and clerks answer to the nurses, the nurses answer to the doctors, the doctors answer to the scientists, the scientists answer to the Rebal generals, and the Rebal generals finally answer to the twelve scientists, only now, they only answer to Blade," Reece explained.

"That's a really complex system," I remarked.

"It's worked quite well in fact for the Rebal, until now at least. There was never a law that stated that one of the twelve scientists answer to another," Reece said. "All the scientists are respected as if they each hold the same amount of power, even though we know that's not the case," Reece added.

"Aha!" he said after another minute of clicking and scrolling. "The prisoner locations."

Ava and I stuck our heads in to get a closer look. "Why would they leave the prisoner page for everyone to see?" Ava asked.

"He had to get through a firewall to get here. Reece here was trained to hack," Morri said with pride.

"You say it like you're the one who can hack," I retorted.

"I can. Blade trained me before I was thrown in the cell. Big mistake," Morri snickered.

"I wonder how mad he is right now," Ava laughed.

"Let's focus, guys," I said, interrupting them.

"Right," Morri said seriously.

"What's your family last name?" Reece questioned.

"Tone," I said.

Reece typed it in the search bar, and only four prisoners popped onto the screen.

"Sorry, Noah," Morri said sympathetically.

I only saw Mom, Dad, Levi, and Anna on the screen. Blade must've turned Seth, Jesi, and John to his side. The thought made me sick.

I put on a straight face.

"We'll find all of them, somehow," I said hopefully.

"Noah, listen. They could be anywhere on earth right now. We would have to search the entire world for them. And if they're with the Rebal, they're probably being protected themselves. No danger is after them, but your family members that are locked up right now need your help. You're gonna have to find John possibly last," Reece explained.

I didn't answer.

"Noah, you have to listen to me. Don't make the same mistake I did," Reece said.

"All right," I said in defeat. "But I'm not going to let Blade get away with this," I growled.

Reece smiled. "I know you won't."

Bang! Bang! Bang! Someone was knocking on the front door next to us.

"Hurry! Go hide in your rooms!" Reece ordered, taking out a pistol.

We didn't object. Ava, Morri and I dove into my room, expecting the worst.

"What are we going to do?" Morri cried.

"What if it's not the Rebal?" Ava asked, hope in her voice.

"Who else would it be?" I said.

The reality of my words sank in, and Ava's face blanched.

I ran to the dresser and motioned for Morri and Ava to come help me.

"We've got to buy ourselves time!" I insisted.

"Barricade the door?" Morri asked.

"It's the least we could do!" Ava yelled.

We all grunted as we pushed the dresser toward the door. Before it got there, Ava ran around to the door and locked it, then we placed the dresser in front of the door.

"Hopefully bullets don't penetrate it," Morri joked.

"How can you not be serious at a time like this!" Ava sneered.

Crack! The sound of wood splintering filled the room. Ava grabbed on to me, whimpering. Morri's face went pale.

Suddenly a fist smashed through the dresser. Ava screamed, and I nearly fainted.

"W-who is tha-that?" Morri stammered.

Foom! The dresser came spiraling toward us, and I brought the girls down to the ground with me just in time before it hit us.

Crash! The wood burst into a thousand pieces behind me. I took a peek behind me and saw a hole at least five feet tall in the wall behind us. How hard did they train the guards in Rebal?

I could feel Ava's short, quick breaths on the back of my neck, and she was clinging to me so hard that I thought my ribs would snap.

Morri was shivering next to me, barely a hint of life in her eyes.

"Would you scaredy cats get off the ground?" a deep voice laughed.

"You almost killed them, Zack!" Jane said.

I looked up and saw her smack his face.

"Ow," Zack said, rubbing his cheek.

I couldn't believe our luck. Had Zack and the others beat the Rebal?

I stifled a grateful laugh, even though all we'd been through was still fresh in my mind. Morri's eyes darted between Jane and Zack. And Ava looked alert as ever.

I stood the girls up and took a step toward Zack.

"That was cool, dude. But make sure that you won't kill us," I said.

"I thought that there were guards in here. Sorry," Zack said.

"You'd better be sorry!" Jane yelled.

"C'mon, Jane! It was an accident!" Zack whined.

"Sorry, guys. I'll talk to him tonight!" Jane grabbed Zack's ear and pulled him out of the room.

"Ow! Ow! Ow!" Zack cried as he left.

I looked at Ava, then at Morri, and laughed. They started to laugh along with me until Ava spoke up.

"I thought we were dead!" She laughed.

"Well, at least they beat the Rebal," I said happily.

"The Rebal never gives up a battle that easy," Morri said suspiciously. "Something's fishy."

"We should just be glad," I said after the laughing stopped.

"Let's go see what happened," Ava suggested. She let go of me and was almost out of the door when a blur zoomed past our room.

"Whoa!" Ava yelped as she fell back. I ran up and caught her before she hit the ground. I looked out the doorway to see Jayce at the table, laughing.

I decided to let it go. He was too bright to be taught a lesson. He'd probably just go past faster next time.

Ava glared at him, and suddenly he started to float.

"Whoa! What's going on!" Jayce said drastically. He clawed at the air around him and started to try to flap down like a bird. Everyone laughed, and he suddenly fell to the ground with a thump.

"Ouch!" he yelled as he grabbed his head in pain.

I looked at Ava and smiled. That was the first time I saw her power in action, and it was awesome.

"Fine! I won't do it anymore!" Jayce grumbled as he walked toward the door.

Ava, Morri, and I walked toward the door to see what all the commotion was about.

As we neared the door, Reece looked at us gratefully and turned to a mysterious man in a gray-and-black suit with multiple layers of armor that was loaded with all sorts of weapons. Was the SWAT team here?

"See! We have everyone!" Reece yelled at the man. Behind him were more figures with the same suits on but with different weapons.

On each of their arms was the yellow triangle symbol with a circle on every corner. Could it be?

"Very good," the man said. "Tone, Jones, and Thresh, check," the man said, scribbling on a clipboard.

"What's going on?" I asked Reece.

"The Tripartite is here," he growled.

CHAPTER 25

Friend or Foe
Noah Tone

My senses suddenly sharpened.

"What?" I asked.

"They came here to check you off," Reece mocked.

"How'd they know we had escaped?" I asked.

"I don't know—" Reece started.

"We knew you escaped from the start," the man at the doorway cut off.

Reece glared at him.

"The Rebal still believe that we are on their side, so they inform us about everything that goes on. And as far as tracking goes, we stole the last location of your tracking devices and assumed from there that you found shelter with the SWR. We know a lot more than the Rebal," the man said.

"What's your name?" I asked the man.

"Call me Agent Brock," he said, extending his hand.

I didn't take it. This was the man that had helped kidnap my family.

"Brock! Where's my family!" I yelled.

Brock pulled his hand back and took in a sharp breath.

"It seems we're in luck. At first we thought that we would have to take the youth by force, but now that we know that they trust you, we can finish this without any problems. By the way, I was an undercover agent hacking and thwarting Blade's plans. You should be proud of me, Tone," Brock exhaled.

"You mean you are going to take us, like you took Noah's family?" Ava exploded.

"It's just a road trip, sister," Brock explained. "You can trust us. We're on your side."

"You may be against Blade, but that doesn't mean we're friends," Ava protested.

"It seems you don't have a choice. We've already made the arrangements long before we found you," Brock replied.

"We're not going until we have some questions answered," I said sternly.

Jane and Zack walked behind us.

"What's going on?" Jane asked.

Brock's face turned alert. I could literally smell his fear.

"We can do this easily or the hard way. I don't think either of us wants this to escalate. Take it from Reece," Brock said shakily. The armed men behind him raised their weapons toward us, anticipating resistance.

All of us turned to Reece for an answer. Even Jayce was serious.

After a moment, Reece sighed out.

"You have to go," Reece blurted out.

"What? No!" Morri shouted.

"I can't risk one of you getting hurt, and on top of that, I'd be blamed for the incident!" Reece shouted back. "Morri, you have to go," he said softer.

Morri blanched. "No, Reece…you can't leave me," she said. "You're the closest thing to family I have left."

Reece trapped her in a hug then finally released her and said, "We'll see each other soon, you'll see," tearing up.

Morri started to cry.

I turned and glared at Brock.

"Now are you happy! You'd better tell me where my family is before I blast your head off!" I blurted out.

"Just doing my job. By the way, they never tell the abductors where they locate the powers for this very reason. But I'm sure Parkins will help you in rescuing your parents. He'll do anything for you if you're on his side," he said plainly.

"Will, will you put us in cells?" Jane asked.

"We're not like the Rebal," Brock replied.

"Then who are you like?" Zack spoke up.

Brock hesitated then said, "Just get in the car!"

As we were walking away, Jayce had to pull Morri to the car with him. Morri fought him the whole way, kicking and screaming.

"No!" Morri screeched.

"You guys are gonna blow our cover!" one of the men complained.

We were getting in the car when a man shoved Ava and me further into the seats. They might not be like the Rebal, but they didn't come across at the moment as nice. These people literally had Reece on the leash, and there was nothing he could do about it.

Ava grabbed my arm, bringing me back into reality.

"What about the plan?" she asked.

I suddenly remembered, the plan!

How are we going to be able to find my family while we were driving to who knows where? I thought, panicked.

The door slammed shut. There was no turning back now, and no one would dare use their powers. One enemy was enough to deal with. And nobody here planned on making more.

"We're just gonna have to see what happens," I told Ava.

"What if they're lying? What if they do treat us like the Rebal did?" Ava whispered, terrified.

"I have a feeling that these people could become a plus in our plan, not a minus. Maybe they know where my family members are since they can communicate with the Rebal," I said hopefully.

"That's a big maybe," Ava replied.

Deep in my mind I knew she was right. Who could we possibly trust right now?

Morri was finally pushed into the front of the car. I couldn't even tell what color or type the car was because the night's darkness swallowed everything up.

Morri was gasping and whimpering as she was shoved into the car. Jayce propped her head on his shoulder and comforted her.

I couldn't imagine what Morri felt right now. Reece, after all, was the only thing she had left, and she was taken away from him without hesitation. Who could imagine her misfortune? She didn't even get the chance to say goodbye.

As Brock stepped inside the car, I asked him, "Where are we going?"

"It's a surprise!" he grunted, clearly angry.

There was nothing we could do but wait now. And hope for the best.

Part Six

CHAPTER 26

Followed
Noah Tone

I grunted as the car jerked to the right. It was the first time we had moved a different direction since hitting the road, and Morri was still sobbing after around an hour. As the car veered, I slammed into Ava, who was sitting to the right of me.

The sudden change in movement startled her awake, and she yawned and stretched.

"Where are we?" she said tiredly.

"Who knows," I replied.

We couldn't look out the side windows because they were tinted down to a pitch-black. I guess security was tight in the Tripartite as well.

Me and Ava had to look out the windshield to get a better look at our surroundings.

In front of us stood a road block. When we neared closer to the checkpoint, I saw a soldier on the curb and a soldier in a small station next to the road that activated the block to open or close. We all saw the Tripartite symbol embedded on the soldiers right arms, like all the rest of the Tripartite.

"State your business," the soldier next to the curb ordered.

"Agent Brock, delivering classified information, level ten," Brock replied, almost bored.

The soldier suddenly shot to attention.

"Sir, understood, sir!" the soldier said in the deepest voice he could muster.

He turned and gave a thumbs-up to the man in the small station.

The man in the station pushed a button, and the block started to slowly open.

For some reason, the block stopped opening and started to close suddenly. Everyone cast around nervous glances.

"What's going on?" Jayce asked, scared.

Brock and his comrades turned and looked out the rearview window of the car.

"We've got company, sir," a large Tripartite soldier in the back with me and Ava said.

"Who is it?" Brock asked, still squinting at the vehicle coming toward us.

Ava and I looked back at the vehicle to get a better look at it. The shark fin symbol swallowed up by a red circle gave the unmistakable and deadly symbol a clear look to all who laid eyes on it.

"It can't be...," Ava whispered.

"The Rebal," I said coldly.

CHAPTER 27

The War Begins
Noah Tone

Brock swung around immediately.

"What!" he yelled.

"You heard him!" Zack replied, standing at attention.

Brock and all his comrades pulled a string on their Tripartite symbols, and suddenly they were replaced with the blood-red shark fins of the Rebal.

"You're spies!" Jayce screamed in alarm.

"Just play along with us, coward!" Brock growled at Jayce.

"Get in the back, all of you!" a large man roared.

Jayce, Jane, Morri, and Zack jumped into the back with Ava and I. Not a moment sooner did the dark Rebal van pull up next to us.

Brock rolled down his window, his arm hanging out and the Rebal symbol easy to see.

The black van's window next to Brock rolled down, and a square-faced tan man with a huge sneer was staring straight at Brock.

"Out of the way, soldier! Official Rebal business. Level three on the way!" the man fired at us.

"Same for us. We have level three fugitives," Brock said coolly.

"Ah, I see," the man in the van started. He opened the door, revealing a chest full of medals and numberless badges.

Jayce gulped as he stepped by the car, right in Brock's face.

"Is your name not Agent Brock?" the man said with distaste.

"Yes…is there something you want?" Brock said uneasily.

"Blade has ordered me to find your location and see what progress you've made, but by the looks of things, it seems that you already have the powers with you. We'll take them from here," the man ordered.

"That won't be necessary, thank you very muc,." Brock said quickly.

"I think it is necessary. I have been given orders, and you are going the opposite direction of Rebal International. Your roads are mixed up, private," the man sneered.

Brock turned red in the face and swallowed.

"And as far as being a general goes, I don't believe that there was a road block here last week, do you?" the man said, eyeing the road block guard.

Sweat beaded down the soldier in the roadblock's face.

The general motioned for his soldiers to get us out. I couldn't believe it. After everything we've been through, it had come to this.

"What are we going to do?" Jane asked, desperation in her voice.

"We'll fight," Zack said.

I looked over everybody.

"We fight," I replied.

Everybody turned serious. Ava's fingers squeezed my hand tightly. It was now or never.

The soldiers were just about to open up the door when Brock broke the deathly silence.

"Stop! General, stop!" he ordered.

The general spun around and screamed, "What now?"

"You're right about me not succeeding my mission," Brock started.

The general raised an eyebrow.

"But if anyone's mixed up, sir, it's you," Brock said coldly, pulling the string again and revealing the Tripartite symbol.

"What the—" the general started.

Pow! Pow! Pow!

The general fell to the ground instantly, three holes through his chest.

"Open fire!" a Rebal soldier roared.

Pak! Pak! Pak! Pak! Pak! The sound of gunfire echoed in the air.

"Go!" I shouted and kicked open the door.

The team and I spilled out in less than a second, and before any of us could even draw a breath, gunfire sprang up all around us. We were everyone's target now.

"Duck!" Morri screamed, but it was too late.

Jane fell against the pavement first, followed by Jayce and Zack.

"No!" Ava yelled and rushed to Jane's side.

Blam! My ears started ringing, and I knew that a bullet had come close to hitting me. I ducked and started to crawl next to Jayce. I was almost there when he turned and grimaced in pain. He was hurt, but not too bad. I knelt over him and saw a gash in his arm. The bullet had luckily grazed him. I focused once more on the battle and saw that Sipes and the rest of the team had the Rebal forces behind the van. They had driven them away from us. Maybe we were wrong about them being the bad guys.

"Rrrrr," Jayce groaned. I turned my focus to him again and saw that he was losing a lot of blood. I tore off a piece of my shirt and wrapped it tightly around his arm.

"Gahhh!" Jayce sputtered. It hurt, and even though I was no doctor, I knew I had to stop the blood.

"You okay?" I asked. Jayce looked up and nodded his head quickly.

I turned and saw that Jane hadn't had such luck. She was unconscious, and a pool of blood was forming around her. Zack was kneeling beside her, a frantic look on his face, while Ava tended to her wound.

Jayce slowly stood up and faced me.

"We have to do something," Jayce said through gritted teeth.

"You're right," I said.

"They have probably already sent a signal to Rebal International. Soldiers will be flooding the place soon," Morri spoke up as she walked over to us.

"Then we'll have to end this quick," I said.

A soldier started running toward us. Soon more followed. When Brock reached us, he turned me around to face him. "You have to get out, now! They're setting up a missile launcher behind the van!"

"So time to go!" Jayce replied, panic in his voice.

"Kid! What do you think you're doing?" Brock screamed as he turned around.

I looked around Brock to see what was going on.

Zack was charging straight at the van.

He was furious. Jane getting hurt must've been the last straw for him, but there was nothing we could do to stop him now.

Foom! Zack's impact with the Rebal van nearly sent a ripple through the earth. The van flew twenty feet backward and landed with a thud in the nearby valley. Then as if in slow motion, a huge explosion erupted in the van. The missile had gone off. Still, Zack charged the now-destroyed van and jumped on it then started tearing the remains apart. The survivors of the wreck gathered around us, weapons drawn. With Zack scouring the wreckage, no one was prepared to face them.

"Put your hands in the air!" one of them ordered.

"You heard the man," Sipes told his men. They all raised their hands one by one, dropping their weapons.

Suddenly the Rebal soldiers' weapons started to rise, slowly at first, but then faster going upward. They struggled to keep them down, and soon they were floating in the air, dangling on their own weapons. I turned to Ava and smiled. It was our turn to fight.

"Now!" I shouted.

Jayce went supersonic and ran past all the soldiers faster than you could blink. He returned with all their pistols and dropped them at Brock's feet.

I smiled and ran into battle.

Jayce continued to unarm soldiers, while Morri tended to Jane. I was just about to jump into battle when I heard something in the distance. I enhanced my hearing and heard the rumble of an engine. The Rebal were coming with more forces. Morri had been right. I turned and focused my attention to the road, and no sooner three black Rebal vans appeared at the top of the hill.

I closed my eyes and concentrated hard on building up vibrations, then when the vans were about ten feet away from me, I pulsed.

The Rebal vans instantly changed direction, going from forward to backward in the matter of a millisecond. Some of the windows flew off before the vans even hit the ground. The survivors of the crashes spilled out of the vans, most of them injured and bleeding out.

Pang! Pow! Pow! There were still those able to fight though. I ducked and pulsed again, flinging the vans another ten feet backward, and the gunfire finally stopped. Then all of a sudden, the van started to rise off the ground. I knew immediately it was Ava. When the van was raised high enough, I could see her. I yelled, "Did you take care of the others back at the car?"

She smiled and nodded. I turned around and saw that the men were on the ground now, flattened like paper. This was what Ava meant when she said she increased the gravitational pull. It was pretty ugly to be honest, but it worked. I turned and motioned for her to drop the van. It came crashing down no sooner. Ava walked around the wreckage, and I met her on the other side.

"We should get out of here. I doubt that's all the reinforcements their sending to us," I explained.

"What about Zack?" Ava asked, pointing to him bent over the exploded Rebal van.

"I think Jane or Morri needs to take care of that," I replied.

I took her hand and said, "Nice fighting out there. We really needed you."

"Not as much as we needed you, though," she replied.

She'd been through nearly everything with me, and still it was like we barely knew each other.

"I still wish we were back at home, to be honest. Even though we're on a huge mission and it's like were in an action movie and all," I said as we were walking back to the car.

"It's crazy that a small team like ours is trying to stop a worldwide threat." She laughed dryly.

"That makes it all the more embarrassing for Blade!" I laughed.

Ava's eyes twinkled, and she laughed back.

We spilled into the car fast because we never knew when the Rebal would decide to strike again. If what Reece had said was right, then the war between the Tripartite and the Rebal had just begun.

CHAPTER 28

A New Threat
Blade Mercantile

Blade sat at his desk, fidgeting with his watch, and longed for some good news for once. Everything was going under, and he, the dictator of the Rebal organization, was sitting here literally watching it happen. World domination was nearly in his grasp when the unlucky escape of Tone and his comrades had taken place, and on top of that, Dr. Parkins was either refusing or unable to send resources to Blade at the time, the Russian compounds were nearly out of fuel, and his power was merely mingling at this point. Oh, how had it come to this, and at this time? His misfortune almost seemed coincidental, actually, too coincidental to seem true.

"May I come in, sir?" a faint voice said from the other side of his door.

Yes! The news on the capture of Tone and the other powers are about to come! Blade thought. He couldn't wait to hear of their failure. He almost wished they were all dead from the strike.

"Yes, come in, please," Blade said almost threateningly.

The door slowly opened, and a Rebal soldier with a gash across his forehead and his uniform torn apart stepped into the room. Normally, you would be punished for such untidiness in the presence of a Rebal leader, but even he cut the man some slack after they had just returned from battle.

The soldier swallowed slowly as he eased himself into the chair facing Blade.

"So how did it go?" Blade said, nearly happy.

"Well, uh—" the soldier started.

"Oh, you don't have to make Tone and his escapees look so bad now, do we? Just tell me what really happened," Blade cut him off.

The soldier laughed uneasily, and Blade's anger began to escalate.

"You failed?" Blade asked.

"Well, uh, sir, you see—" the soldier started.

"I've seen everything! I can't stand one more failed mission, so help me I'll slit one of your throats!" Blade screamed.

"They were powers, sir!" the soldier said defensively.

"Yes, untrained powers, and you are trained soldiers! Can the embarrassment be any worse!" Blade yelled back. "Shouldn't Brock be reporting to me?" Blade added in fury.

The soldier turned red in the face. "Sir, Brock, has…turned," he explained.

"You mean he's turned…against me?" Blade asked, quieter this time.

"Yes, sir, and many others were with him, not including the powers," the soldier explained.

Blade looked up at the ceiling. "You don't say," he whispered. "Locate his coordinates," Blade ordered.

"Sir, he doesn't have any coordinates," the soldier replied.

"You mean, he doesn't have a tracking device implant?" Blade asked.

"He never had one. His identity doesn't even state that he reports or works at Rebal International. He works at Capitol 1 International," the soldier explained.

"In Kansas?" Blade asked, his voice rising.

"Yes, sir," the soldier replied.

"Well, well, well…rebels," Blade said, savoring the words.

"They also wore a symbol that looked like this," the soldier said, handing him a picture of a black triangle connecting three dots encased in a yellow circle.

"Parkins's calling card," Blade whispered, the pieces of the puzzle coming together. "You may leave. The powers are of no interest to us at the moment any longer. We've got a bigger problem on our hands at the moment," Blade ordered.

Once the soldier left the room, Blade smiled to himself.

"Oh, poor, poor Parkins. I'm afraid that he'll see what jealousy gets him." Blade laughed.

He turned on his holographic map and lit a match, setting it on the United States. "It seems that world domination is in fact on our side. We will overrun the world while at the same time destroy the Tripartite as they get in our way. Nothing will stop us, and I will have revenge." Blade cackled. He laughed maniacally as the fire spread to Canada and South America. Soon the Tripartite's dream would be their fate.

CHAPTER 29

Trip to Freedom
Morri Thresh

Morri groggily sat up, still dazed after the Rebal attack and being taken away from Reece. It had all happened so fast, her whole world gone.

A sick sensation suddenly boiled in her belly, and she opened her eyes to see miles and miles of light-blue water out of a circular window. Where were they?

Morri turned and saw Jayce in the seat next to her, reading a book quietly.

"Seasick?" he asked.

"I never knew I could get seasick, not until now, at least." She yawned. Her eyes were still puffy from screaming and crying.

"We're on a boat, by the way," Jayce added.

"Even someone as dumb as you could figure that out," Morri joked.

"I had to carry you onto the boat. You should be thanking me, sweetie," Jayce fired at her.

"Awww, was I too heavy for you?" she said sarcastically.

"Yeah, what have you been eating anyway?" Jayce laughed.

"Shut up," she sneered.

Her and Jayce had an odd relationship, both of them being the jokesters in the group, although she didn't know if Jayce even meant to be funny, because most of the time he was just being his childish self. The only reason she was ever funny was to hide the pain. It made Morri look stronger emotionally than what she really was. Being taken away from Reece had unleashed her true feelings. Now there was no one left whom she loved, no one left who loved her.

Morri didn't love Reece like she wanted to marry him. He was more like a father to her. After Morri's parents passed away, she never even knew them much, Morri was only five when she was taken, and barely even remembered anything about them. The hurt comes from the loneliness she felt when she was an outcast that no one cared about. Morri felt lucky to be brought along as it is, with everyone else having level three and two powers, and her the only level one in the whole group.

Having Reece taken away from her was easily the worst thing that had ever happened to her. Being locked up in a cell your whole life, nothing much really happens to you.

Morri still felt like telling the gang the truth about why she was thrown into the cell, the true reason she was useless, or more a threat to the Rebal.

"Morri!" Jane said as she wrapped her in a hug. Morri didn't resist. Jane was the only understanding person in the cells while she was alone. She knew emotions well. She only wished she knew how to treat them.

Morri had to admit that she always envied Jane back in the cell as she had her own boyfriend to keep her company. Morri couldn't imagine their luck being thrown in together.

Jayce always seemed to be the easygoing one, but she always sensed he had a mixed past behind that smile. Zack was the serious one, the protector, the leader. His ability to always be alert, actually, to be honest, scared her. Jane was the compassionate one, the healer, a ray of sunshine in their ever-darkening days in the wet, dark, cold miserable cells. Morri honestly didn't know how long they could have lasted in there if Noah and Ava hadn't come to their rescue.

Noah was like the intruder, immediately taking Zack's place as leader and sending him down in the ranks. Not that it seemed like Zack really cared. Noah was a great leader. Ava was hard to figure out, sometimes happy, sometimes sad, sometimes angry, sometimes giddy with excitement. Her personality was one that was hard to come by.

"Hi, Jane," she replied.

"Don't worry, Reece is with the Tripartite. I'm sure he'll make visits," Jane reassured her.

"I only can hope that the Rebal haven't hunted him down already," Morri replied, a sudden feeling of dread overwhelming her.

What if they did find him? What if he's, he's…

No, ot couldn't be. The whole Tripartite would've responded to an attack, wouldn't they?

Morri's thoughts were lost by Jane's voice. "Morri? Morri, are you all right?"

She suddenly slipped back into reality.

"Yeah, yeah, I'm all right," she said quickly.

"You looked like you were a million miles away," Jane replied.

"I know that look," Zack said walking up next to her. "What's on your mind?"

"Nothing. It's just everything that's happened, you know," Morri said unconvincingly.

Zack and Jane exchanged a look that told her they knew she was lying. Thankfully they didn't push her about it.

"Just tell us if you need any help, all right?" Jane said soothingly.

"Not if she throws up in a bucket first," Jayce snickered.

Jane shot daggers at him.

"What? The waves are pretty choppy!" Jayce said innocently.

Zack rolled his eyes and walked Jane out of the room, leaving Morri and the joker alone again.

"I really am sorry, though," Jayce said.

"That's not a lot coming from you," she huffed.

"I know a thing or two about what you're going through," Jayce added.

"Oh, really? What?" Morri shot at him.

"Uh, nothing. It's nothing really. Doesn't matter anymore," Jayce said fast, shaking his head as if to forget something.

Morri didn't know what, but there was something about Jayce that's was different, secretive. She guessed she'd just have to wait to find out what it is. In the meantime, she'd have to figure out where they were in the first place.

"I'm going to check around the bow," she lied, standing up from her seat.

"Need a barf bag?" Jayce smirked.

"I'll pass," Morri said darkly as she let the door close behind her.

The bow was small, for a boat at least. There were two Tripartite sailormen standing near the railing, like they could guard them from a battleship or something.

There was a door to either side of the room her and Jayce were in. She just had to figure out where the captain was.

Morri peered through the door to her right and saw Ava and Jane talking, while Zack and Noah played cards on the opposite wall.

How can they be so calm at a time like this? Not even knowing where they are going? she thought. Was there something Morri didn't know? Being Morri, that sounded like a silly question, since she was basically a walking search bar, but at the same time it felt wrong to keep information from a computer. Maybe they don't trust her because of her power, like Blade did. The thought made her consider jumping overboard and swimming back to Reece, but the idea was too absurd to even think about for long.

Morri walked to the other door and saw a nurse in it, who was tending to a small figure, a child maybe? She didn't take the time to figure out who it was. She was too busy thinking about why no one was steering the boat in the first place.

Morri looked up and suddenly didn't feel that smart. Of course! Most boats operate from the top floor. She hadn't even thought about this boat having one.

Morri climbed up a ramp and knocked on the shiny white door. This one was different from the others, it having a golden buoy design around the circle window. The door opened not a minute later, and she was met by a tan-skinned man with golden flowing hair and a perfect smile. He'd be enough to make any lady fall in love with him at first sight. The way his muscles rippled throughout his whole body and even showed through his uniform made him a total knockout.

"Is there something you want, miss?" the man said a little too cheerfully.

"Uh, uh." The sight of him had made Morri lose her breath. She was lucky he saved her just then.

"Of course, please excuse my manners, ma'am, but my name is Captain Flint, at your service!" he said brightly, extending his hand.

Morri shook it, and his grip nearly crushed her fingers.

"Uh, of course," she said while he pulled her into the room. Everywhere there were nets hanging on the wall, and the head of a swordfish even suck out of the wall to the left of her.

"Direct orders from the boss told me that I must pay special respect to you and your comrades, not that I appreciate the order, but I'd give my time to any lady as lovely as you," Flint said casually.

Morri couldn't help blushing. No boy had ever talked to her like that.

"Yes, well, I was wondering where we were in the first place," she forced out.

"Of course! Right now were right about in the Atlantic Ocean, close to the New York Coast, as a matter of fact," Flint said cheerfully.

"Why are we going to the New York coast?" she asked.

"To get you into Alliance safety, of course. We wouldn't want you over in Europe, where the Rebal have power," Flint explained.

"I didn't realize how long I'd been out," Morri said in surprise.

"Ah, it's hard for us captains to carry out orders as it is anyway. It's easy to soon think you command an entire navy," Flint joked.

"It was nice meeting you, Flint," Morri added before walking out of the door. Once she closed it, she sighed. Not only was he handsome, he was also charming.

Don't get caught up with yourself. He probably already has a family. Morri scolded herself.

She walked back down to where the nurse's door was and saw the small figure lying on the bed. Was he or she injured, dead even? Morri decided to ask the others.

She rushed to the door that the gang was grouped in and opened it quickly.

Ava immediately stood. "Is there anything wrong?" she said, alert in her voice.

"Oh, no. I was just wondering who the person in the nurse's office was," Morri asked.

"Oh, him," Zack said quietly.

"We found him stranded on the dock that this boat was held on. He claimed to have escaped the Rebal, and he's a level one power," Jane explained.

"Really?" she said.

"You can never really trust someone at first. We only know what he's told us," Jane replied.

"What's his power anyway?" Morri questioned.

"We figured out fast. The moment he saw Brock and the rest of his team of commandos, he shot up the side of a building. Their fake Rebal symbol must have freaked him out," Jayce said out of nowhere.

She spun around, startled. She didn't know he'd entered the room right now. Morri glared at him, but he just smiled back at her. She huffed and sat in the seat next to Zack.

"Did I hear you right? Jayce just said he went up the building," Morri asked.

"He sure did. I had to shoot him down with a wave of vibrations to capture him. He's small, but fast," Noah spoke up.

"He has superclimbing powers?" she said in wonder.

"Yeah, looks like we've got Spide-Man on board!" Zack laughed.

"We aren't sure if we can trust him, though. The second he fell to the ground, he nearly blacked out. He barely told us anything before he went unconscious," Ava explained.

Morri never thought there would be another level one in this gang, but maybe she was wrong. She definitely felt like she'd earned a rank higher, though.

Suddenly the boat lurched to a stop. Ava and Jayce hit to the floor, as if expecting a Navy battleship to pull up next to them and rip them to pieces, but Morri couldn't blame them after all they've been through.

Ava lifted her head a bit and said, "What's going on, guys?"

Morri, Noah, and Zack ran out to the dock and looked at their surroundings. Ahead of us stood a gleaming city. Toward the middle of the magnificent city, a skyscraper stood above all the rest, the Empire State building. Morri looked behind her, and the iconic Statue of Liberty was facing them. They were here. They'd finally made it to the Alliance.

Chapter 30

The Alliance
Morri Thresh

"Welcome to New York," Noah announced as they stepped back inside the cabin.

"New York?" Ava said, confused.

"If the Alliance captured us in the first place, they were bound to take us back to the United States. We are home. Or at least close to it," Noah explained, avoiding Zack and Jane's gazes. They were still as far from ever from anything to even call a home.

"So we're safe then?" Jayce spoke up, mustering as much courage as he could.

"Yes, we're safe," Morri assured him.

"Or far from it," Zack put out. "The Rebal could've set a spy on this ship. We could be tracked for all we know," Zack added, settling the fear back into everyone.

"I think it's time we figured out who that kid really is," Morri said.

Everybody nodded their heads in agreement. All secrets were to be revealed, especially if their lives depended on it.

Once they walked outside onto the bow, a dock was straight ahead of them. They were going to dock, then they should be safe, safe from Blade and the Rebal. Back then in the cell, escape seemed hopeless, let alone freedom.

Once they stepped onto the dock, Morri felt a sensation of courage lift her up. They had beaten Blade—she had beaten Blade. Now that they were safe, they could leave that cruel world behind them. Even though Noah still wanted to go back and defeat Blade, all of them knew that Noah wouldn't succeed.

Morri had planned on bailing out whenever he asked them to go back. She had a feeling most of the rest of them would do the same.

The most they could do was wish him luck and remember what he'd done for them, for they knew Noah wouldn't return.

Morri turned her attention back to the magnificent city standing before them. New York, her birthplace. She expected to have felt some kind of connection to the place, but after all these years it was just a distant memory by now.

"Do you think your parents are still here?" Jane whispered as she met her on the dock.

Morri thought over her words. There could be a chance. Not that she didn't want to find them. It was getting involved with the Rebal that worried her. Morri didn't want to finally find where they were and find corpses.

"The time will come when I will look for them, but for now I'll stay out of any missions for a while," Morri replied.

Jane nodded her head as if she understood. She knew how being in that cell could break you. She suddenly grimaced and almost fell. Morri had to steady her so she'd stay on her feet.

"What's wrong?" Morri asked.

"The Rebal, they shot me, remember?" Jane replied through gritted teeth.

"Oh! Are you okay?" she said, panicked.

"Yeah, they took care of it on the ship, but the pain keeps coming back," Jane explained then reached into her pocket and pulled out a canister. She screwed the cap off and took a pill out then popped it into her mouth. An Advil. Morri helped her screw on the lid, and she shoved it back into her pocket.

Brock stepped off the boat and stood in front of them, counting them over like one of them was lost or something. When he felt sure that they were all there, he motioned to one of his agents. The agent grabbed the small child that had been in the nursing office by the arm and walked him over to Brock. Brock laid his hand on the boy's shoulder.

"This here is Kaleb. We have been given strict orders to bring him with you to the Alliance headquarters. The Alliance counsel will determine whether or not he will aid you in your given mission. You are to treat him fairly and with respect. Anyone with objections will answer to me," he said coldly.

Morri and the others cast one another nervous looks. They hadn't even met the kid, and the Alliance was already promoting him on their team.

He turned on his heels and marched forward off the dock, waiting for them was an armored vehicle with a large turret on the top. Not something you would usually see in New York.

Kaleb tagged along after them, falling behind in the back. Being left out wasn't fun. Morri would know. Him being on their team could be the Alliance's worst mistake, but if they gave him a chance, he could be their greatest addition to their team.

They started filing into the armored car. Jayce looked inside of it in awe, like it was the most high-tech thing in the world.

"Won't this attract attention?" Noah asked sternly.

"It is our duty to protect you at all costs. Not that I like the mode of transportation the Alliance sent us, but it could be worse," Brock replied.

"What would you like to ride in, then?" Morri asked.

Brock considered this question for a moment.

"An Abrams tank would've been nice," he said thoughtfully.

They silently laughed as the vehicle took off.

The vehicle sped through the dazzling city of NYC, the hundreds of gleaming glass skyscrapers reflecting off the sunlight. Jayce was too busy looking at the armored car controls to appreciate the wonder of such a powerful and stunning city. Morri suddenly realized that if Blade succeeded in taking over the world, this city would be reduced to rubble. Just the thought was unimaginable. She could only hope that the Tripartite could put down the threat of the Rebal.

The car screeched to a halt, and before them stood a massive skyscraper with the letter *A* broadcasted at the top. This was the Alliance headquarters? Right here in New York City?

"Welcome to New York Defense. The Alliance places a defensive unit in every one of the US states. Blade will have to fight on fifty fronts if a war ever breaks out," Brock explained.

So this wasn't the Alliance headquarters, and it was almost as impressive as the Rebal's headquarters. Blade would have to take second thoughts on declaring war on the Tripartite.

"The states that line the Atlantic coast are fiercely defending. We believe that the Rebal will launch an attack from Europe, but our South American Branch defends the Pacific in case they attack from Asia."

"I can see that you're prepared for anything," Noah commented.

"We try to be, but we're always aware that the Rebal are a force to be reckoned with," Brock said sternly.

Morri, of all people, knew he was right.

When they pulled into the driveway, Brock ordered them to get out and stand in a line. They would walk single file into the defense headquarters, then they would receive instruction from a guide.

"I can only hope that Reece was wrong about them being as bad as the Rebal," Jane whispered.

Morri nodded her head in agreement. If there was one place she would hate to spend the night, it was a cell.

They all obeyed, and once Brock was sure they were all accounted for, he nodded to his agents, and they flanked them on either side.

They slowly started walking toward the skyscraper. The sheer size of it sent chills up Morri's spine. These people held power, power as intimidating as this skyscraper.

Once they stepped through the double glass doors, plain amazement hit her. Soldiers, agents, and special forces were bustling around in full uniform. Many were busy talking over the walkies, and others were huddled around radars and maps, receiving transmissions and yelling orders to random soldiers.

The place looked like it was on full lockdown, but it was on full operation instead.

The tables, chairs, walls, and ceiling were all shiny white, two men in suits guarded the entrance, and a spiral staircase leading up to the next floor was on the other side of the room. The place was so busy the stairway had two lanes. Whatever rebellion those scientists had started was the biggest Morri had ever seen. People looked at them with confused expressions as they passed through the crowd. Morri felt more out of place than she had in her entire life.

Once they finally made it to the front desk, the woman there looked at them and gave the biggest, fakest smile Morri had ever seen.

"Is there something I can do for you, honey?" she said, obviously annoyed.

"They're with me," Brock said.

"Oh, Brock! I was wondering when you'd get back from your mission," she said all dreamy-eyed. She stared at his biceps and met his face again with a giggle.

"Lane, this is very important business," Brock explained.

"Oh, I'll keep the kids here with me if you want," she said happily.

"Actually, the big man wants them in his office," Brock replied in a hurry.

"Oh, oh my! Rebal bugs? Spies!" she said worriedly.

"No, they actually escaped a Rebal prison," Brock said calmly, masking his impatience.

"Oh, the poor babies," Lane said, choking back a sob.

Morri held back from tearing her face off.

"They're powers," Brock said, ending the conversation.

Lane's face suddenly went pale.

"Yep, that's us," Jayce added.

Lane fumbled with her drawers before finally pulling out a dark-red laminated slip with the Tripartite symbol printed on it.

She grabbed her headpiece and shouted into the microphone.

"Grade five meeting to be held in Parkins's office. Now," Lane said seriously.

She handed the slip to Brock and started blushing furiously.

"I'm so sorry for holding you up. We'll talk later," she said embarrassed.

She then stared right at all of them.

"The fate of the war depends on you. Don't fail us."

The next person in line came up to the desk, and no sooner they were heading to an elevator to the right side of the bottom floor.

"What was that all about?" Ava asked as they descended up to the top floor.

"Soon you will see how important you really are," Brock said when the elevator stopped.

Once Morri and the rest of them stepped out of the elevator, a woman in a uniform greeted them.

"I'll be taking you from here," she said smiling.

Morri turned to Brock.

"You're not coming?" she asked.

"No, I have performed my duty. My work is done," he replied, almost sadly.

"What will you do now?" Noah asked.

"Another mission. Most likely in Africa. The Tripartite is trying to expand their borders. I must say, this is the greatest mission I've participated in for a long time," he said longingly. "Thank you," he finished.

"No, thank you," Morri replied.

He gave a half smile and saluted them. The elevator doors closed, and he was gone.

Morri could tell the rest of the gang felt sad, even she did.

The woman led them down a long hall and stopped at two big glass doors. She slid them to the side, and a huge table surrounded by plush couches were set before them.

Three men sat at the table. The one at the head of the table spoke up first.

"Please, take a seat," he said warmly.

They all found an empty seat and settled into the impressively comfortable couches. It took all Morri's effort not to doze off.

"My name is Dr. Parkins," the man at the head of the table said. "Welcome to the Alliance."

Part Seven

Chapter 31

The Opponent
Noah Tone

I couldn't believe what I'd just heard. This was the leader of the Tripartite, the rebel of all rebels.

Are we really this important? I thought to myself.

I saw all the other looks of awe and amazement plastered on the rest of the gang's faces. I was sure mine looked the same.

Dr. Parkins waited, like he wanted us to say something.

"And we're the SGI. The team of powers you heard about," I struggled to say.

"You must be Noah. I've heard a lot about you. Mostly complaints from Blade. You're daring, decisive. That's the type of attributes we need," Parkins said.

"Uh, thank you, sir," I replied, not knowing if that was a compliment.

"Can control sound waves. Level three. Hmmm…very good addition to the Tripartite," Parkins said slowly, reading a clipboard as he talked. "And you?" he said, glancing at Ava, who was sitting next to me.

"Ava, Ava Jones, sir," she stuttered.

He looked back down at his clipboard, nodding his head in approval as he did.

"Gravitational powers. Useful in a number of ways," he said, a hint of excitement in his voice.

Jayce was giddy. Moving all around in his seat and tapping the floor with his shoes.

Parkins looked to him next.

"I believe that you're Jayce," he said, almost bored.

"How'd you know my name?" Jayce asked, the happiness draining from him.

"Wild guess," Parkins continued. "Supersonic speed. I always knew the Flash wasn't just a made-up comic hero," Parkins laughed.

Jayce beamed.

"And, Morri?" Parkins asked, looking around the table.

Morri raised her hand.

"Ah, the prize jewel of them all. Your information and knowledge will aid us greatly," Parkins said happily.

To my surprise, Morri actually smiled.

Zack waited expectantly, blinking and swallowing hard.

"Zack Gupta. A recognizable asset to our chain of commanders. Don't worry, there will be plenty of missions for you," Parkins said seriously.

Zack's shoulders slumped.

"And finally, Jane," Parkins said, smiling at her.

"That's me," Jane laughed quietly. It always felt she had come last in everything. I would fix that.

"Very extraordinary power. Show me," Parkins insisted.

Jane blanched but then obeyed. I knew what was wrong. The shot in her stomach had taken away all her energy.

She attempted to disappear again and then gasped, falling into Zack's arms.

"Can you help her?" Zack cried, desperation in his voice.

"What's wrong?" Parkins said, surprised.

"She got shot in the stomach. The Rebal attacked us on our way through Switzerland!" I shouted, standing up so he could see me.

"I'll get a medic right away!" Parkins replied, punching in a dial faster than lightning.

"Medic, meeting room ASAP!" Parkins yelled into the phone.

He slid the phone back into his pocket.

"I'm so sorry," Parkins apologized.

"It's not your fault. You didn't know," Ava reassured him.

"No, it is my fault. I should've known what condition she was in before we met. An injured soldier is an army's worst weakness," Parkins replied.

His wording was odd. He should be worried about the person, Jane. Not the soldier he saw her as.

The glass doors burst open, and two nurses, with a Red Cross armband on their right arms, rushed in with a stretcher. Zack laid her on the stretcher and attempted to follow her outside. The door shut in front of him, and he leaned against the door, his face twisted in concern.

"I'm sorry, I have to go with her," Zack said to Parkins.

"I'm sorry, but you'll have to stay here. We have a lot to discuss," Parkins replied.

Zack slammed his fist on the table.

"I'm going to go with her! Did you not hear what I just said?" he roared.

"I can assure you that our nurses are the best you will find. Your friend will be fine," Parkins said seriously, as if daring Zack to reject him. His eyes were cold and calculating like a robot. It made me feel uneasy.

Zack complied, slowly settling into his seat, but still glared at Parkins.

"I'm not so sure that you're any different than the Rebal," Zack growled.

"Thanks for getting our topic off to a good start!" Parkins beamed, back to his normal self.

Zack glowered.

"But I must say that it's the way you look at things that determines what you think about someone. Take Blade, for example. A power-hungry, corrupt, unpredictable man. He may seem like a terrible leader, but he is a strategic and challenging opponent. I should know. He was my partner. Remember who your opponent is.

Don't forget, or else you will stray into the opponent's trap," Parkins explained.

"Why were you his partner?" I asked.

"Before I chose to lead the trade role, I worked with Blade in medical research. We fought cancer together. We were friends," he said in a distant voice.

"Why did you stop?" Morri asked.

"A promising experiment went terribly wrong. But if that experiment never happened, you wouldn't be here. That experiment created the very first power," Parkins said, a little scared.

"What? Why didn't you get the credit for the experiment?" Ava asked, confused.

"When the experiment went haywire, I got knocked out in all the chaos. When I woke up, the cure was gone, the ingredients for the cure were probably destroyed, and my patient, Emma, was gone," Parkins said darkly.

Ava shifted in her seat next to me. Something he'd said made her feel uncomfortable.

"The only person who knew about the experiment was Blade. He was the only person who could be responsible for it," Parkins seethed. "I had no evidence that he stole the cure. The cameras blacked out before anything could be taped. The only thing that was visible was a raging windstorm tearing the lab apart. It was the most terrifying thing I'd ever witnessed," Parkins said softly.

He brightened up and continued the conversation. "But things always have a twisted past. After all, that experiment made miracles like you. I only wish that Blade hadn't taken most of you," Parkins said with distaste. "But what Blade doesn't understand is that the strongest of the powers turn against him, the strongest refuse to do evil and do good. You are among those few, and I hope that with the help of you and your other kind, the Tripartite will put Blade's threat to an end," Parkins said brightly.

"Blade told us that we didn't know our own potential. What can we do?" I asked.

"Many, many things. Sadly, Blade has brainwashed children and teenagers into using those powers to his advantage." Parkins replied.

I thought back to Jesi, John, and Seth. Were they under Blade's complete control? Were they killing innocent people with their gifts? I couldn't think about it for long. It was too painful.

"Blade always gets what he wants. He never loses," Jayce said in annoyance.

"It may seem like so, but that is surprisingly not true," Parkins replied with excitement in his voice.

"You see. Blade has a flaw."

Chapter 32

Evil's Weakness
Noah Tone

I couldn't believe it. Someone as powerful, as smart, as crafty, as ruthless as Blade could have a flaw, a weakness? It was so extraordinary I never even gave thought to it.

"No way," Jayce said in unbelief.

"Oh, it is very true." Parkins laughed. "After all those years of working with him, I finally found it out," he said, almost bored.

"Well, what is it then?" Ava insisted.

"Please, take it slowly. I know it's a lot to comprehend, but we must go from the start." Parkins laughed.

Everyone listened intently, even Zack.

"You see, evil was from the start, when Cain killed Abel, when slavery began, why, even when the first man set foot on earth. There is always evil with the good, always," Parkins said almost darkly. "But evil is always stopped somehow. One way or another, it's stopped," Parkins said thoughtfully, as if to himself. "The great Egyptian Empire, having corrupt rulers and a huge amount of slaves, not just an empire, an evil empire. When Moses saved the slaves, their downfall was basically set before them. They were stopped," Parkins said in amazement.

"The Roman Empire, turned from democracy to empire, treated people with hatred, stole from people, took money from everyone, persecuted Jews and Christians alike, evil. They fell embarrassingly to barbaric invaders. Quite amazing, isn't it? The Muslim era, such a powerful religion that whole countries fell under its control. They beheaded, killed, dissected, and cursed the bodies and kingdoms of their enemies, believed that world dominance was the only way to appease the gods evil. Weakened by the crusades and eventually reduced to small, weak countries in the Middle East. They were stopped.

"Germany, in WWI and WWII, gaining so much success, capturing enemy lands, bombing, raiding, and wiping out any who dared oppose them, attempting to make the Jews go Extinct. Evil. Amid all their staggering success, somehow the unexplained choice of attacking Russia came into view. Mistakes, failures, and unwise choices eventually lead to their defeat. Stopped again," Parkins said in a hushed tone.

"You see anything in common with all of these great empires and countries?" Parkins asked. "Anyone?"

"They were all evil, and they were all stopped," I said thoughtfully. This was going somewhere. I could feel it.

"Not only that, but they were nearly unstoppable," Parkins explained. "Each one of these evil empires had the shot of taking over the entire world as we know it. But they didn't," Parkins said, a smile spreading across his face. "And you know why they never succeeded?"

"No, why?" Zack asked, obviously bored.

"Because they made choices. Choices that led to their downfall!" Parkins said like it explained everything. "The Egyptian Empire, chasing after the slaves and getting swallowed up by the sea. The Roman Empire, deciding to make no allies, to stay apart from all other civilizations and referring to anyone outside of their empire as Barbarians, eventually these barbarians destroyed their entire empire! The Muslim Empire, recapturing Jerusalem countless times, and getting pushed back each time they succeeded, decided to attack Spain and conquer it! Yet they never stopped attacking, just further weakened their army every time they attacked. Why did they not realize this?" Parkins said thoughtfully. "The Germans, receding the attack on Britain and deciding to attack Russia! Their own ally! Every single one of these choices led to each empire's downfall! But if it led to their downfall, why did they choose to make these choices?" Parkins asked in astonishment.

We were unable to answer that question. My mind was blank.

"I didn't expect you to know. No one does," Parkins laughed. "My guess is that every time an evil force wreaks havoc, there's a limit. A limit of how far it can go," Parkins explained. "No one is going to take over the world. Simply because it would be evil to do it. It wouldn't be possible if it wasn't for a cause," Parkins pointed out. "Each empire had its time. It may now be time for Blade's, but I have a strong feeling that he will face the same fate, the fate of all the great empires before him, the evil empires before him. We are the team that fights for a cause. Blade is the team that fights for a flaw, a flaw they will soon witness themselves," Parkins ended.

"Wow. You really think so?" Morri asked.

"Positive," Parkins assured her.

"Sooo, why are we fighting against him?" Zack asked, annoyed.

"Good and evil must coexist with each other. Without one, there's not the other, or worse, one takes control of the other. We, the US, are the good. Blade and the Rebal are evil. If one side gains too much power, the other takes that power away. It's just simple common sense," Parkins explained. "Without us to stand against Blade, his power would grow too powerful, and no good could take it away from him. We were predestined to face him. It's our role, our job," Parkins told Zack.

Zack was too stunned to reply.

"Do you know when the war will start?" I asked Parkins.

"It already has," Parkins replied.

"Whoa! What are we gonna do?" Jayce panicked.

"Do not fear. The war is over, already won. The next is going to start soon," Parkins assured him.

"What?" Morri replied, confused.

"A battle against Blade has already been fought. I am going to regret telling you the truth, but I sadly fought on the Rebal's side," Parkins said sadly.

"This was before you knew that Blade was evil. It wasn't your fault," I told him.

"I learned a great lesson from that war. That Blade was wrong, was mad about trying to take over the world. I saw him fail, and I didn't want to be on the losing side of another war," Parkins explained. "That's why I commenced my plan to take the other scientists away from him, to form a fighting force of his own men against him. That's why I created the Tripartite."

"Why did we not know about this war?" Zack asked suspiciously.

"It was for your own good,. Knowing about one deadly war might take you out of the next," Parkins explained. "And we need you in this war," he added.

"You're right. I don't want to be in a war," Morri joked.

"I do hope you change your mind after I explain this to you," Parkins replied, picking up a remote and pressing a button.

Suddenly the wall behind us lit up. And a picture of a city on fire appeared on the screen.

"This is Moscow," Parkins explained sadly.

"How did this happen?" I asked in unbelief.

"A power, fire abilities," Parkins said with distaste.

I looked at the left side of the screen and saw a smug-faced teen with a dirty face. He had a red uniform on with a fire symbol badge on his breast pocket. He was the power.

More cities appeared. New York frozen in ice. Beijing completely isolated, only the frames of buildings standing. London getting blasted by wind, and Big Ben's Tower blowing off. Bangkok falling down in a sinkhole. Paris covered in vines and looking like a jungle, and the person, she was…Mom. Tokyo in a lightning storm, with lightning bolts toppling towers. Rio De Janeiro, with towers deformed, bent and curved, and…that person, he looked young, but just like Dad.

Parkins was watery eyed when he turned off the screen and the lights turned back on.

"This, not WWII, was the scariest time in history," Parkins explained.

"How, how did we not know about this?" Ava struggled to say.

"The children were not able to stand the guilt of killing so many lives, a certain power reversed time itself and made everything normal again," Parkins replied.

"When did this happen anyway?" I asked.

"Nineteen ninety-five. Very prior to our time. After the Cold War, Blade saw peace as an opportunity. He knew no one would expect something like this," Parkins continued. "However, unable to bear the guilt of killing innocent lives, the powers turned against Blade and escaped him, leading normal lives in the normal world. Not much is known of how exactly they revolted, but if they hadn't, there may not be a world as we know it."

Now it all made sense, the time, the place, everything. Dad and Mom were in those photos. They had destroyed those cities, had been trained and followed Blade. But they revolted. I knew I could count on my parents to do the right thing. But who reversed time?

Parkins cleared his throat. "You see, Blade, despite his staggering success, was stopped. You may not have witnessed it, but your parents know of evil's weakness, and soon you will too."

Chapter 33

The Mission
Noah Tone

"Why did you show us these things?" Morri asked dryly.

"Because I hoped you would realize what destruction Blade and the Rebal can cause. I wanted you to join the fight so that nothing like this ever happens again. That's why I ran and made the Tripartite—to stop Blade," Parkins explained flatly.

"I am," I spoke up. "I will rescue my family and defeat Blade whatever it takes," I added.

"Me too," Ava said, standing up and slipping her hand into mine. I turned to her and smiled. I knew I could count on her. "If there's a chance that my parents are still alive, I'll find them whatever the cost," she assured Parkins

"Well, there's nothing else I can do anyway," Morri said, standing up too.

I was surprised. I thought she would be the first to reject.

Jayce and Zack stayed down, so did Kaleb.

Parkins looked at Kaleb with interest.

"You've never spoken here yet. I didn't even know you were here," Parkins said in interest.

"I try to stay out of things, especially if it has to do with Blade," Kaleb said darkly.

"You must be the boy that just escaped the Rebal complex in Berlin," Parkins asked.

I was stunned. Berlin, that was halfway across Europe, very far from Switzerland. I couldn't imagine what he'd gone through escaping through a whole Rebal-infested country.

"We can talk over your decision later, Kaleb. I have a feeling you're not telling us everything about your escape or what you've been through," Parkins said coolly.

Kaleb pulled his hood over his head.

"What about you two young men?" Parkins insisted Zack and Jayce. He pointed at Jayce. "I was expecting your hand to go up first, bright boy. You're young and capable of so much. Why are you rejecting the offer?"

Parkins was right. I thought Jayce would volunteer openly and without any fear.

"I, uh, I…just don't feel like it," Jayce said forcefully.

Parkins raised an eyebrow.

"Perhaps I need to talk with you and Kaleb," Parkins said.

"Uh, no, no no no. I think I really just don't want to go into a war. I know it'd be cool to be a hero and all, but, but—" Jayce trailed off.

"But what?" Morri pushed, glaring at him. I felt like she wanted him to go for some reason.

"I'm scared, all right! I try to act cool and funny so no one thinks I'm hurt and feels sorry for me! I wanted to not be in the whole thing the whole time! I wanted to run away! I'm a coward!" he yelled.

Everyone stood in silence and shock.

Why hadn't he told us before? I thought.

"When my parents were taken, I was old enough to know what was going on. I saw them die in front of my own eyes. I've been scared ever since. I hate Blade, but not enough that I'll be brave enough to stand against him. He knows that, and so do I," Jayce said, teary-eyed.

"Please take a seat. I won't force you to go if you don't want to," Parkins said apologetically.

Before Jayce could sit, Morri grabbed his arm.

"Jayce! You don't need to be scared. We are all here for you! I'm here for you." She wrapped her arms around him and started sobbing into his shirt. I saw a tear slide down his cheek, and he put his arms around her.

That was something I definitely wasn't expecting, but it looked like Jayce and Morri were more than friends too. Even Zack, who thought he knew everybody was surprised.

Zack then stood.

"I've always known you, bro. I thought I knew you too. I'm sorry I couldn't help you all that time. But now I will. I've seen the fear and pain Blade has given all of us, and after this I am going to put it to a stop. I-I volunteer to go on your mission. I'll tell Jane about it too," Zack said seriously.

Kaleb still remained seated.

Jayce let go of Morri and sat her down.

"I'll go. I'll be brave as I can, now I know that my team needs me," Jayce said, a new hint of truth in his voice.

"It looks like we have a full team then, well, mostly," Parkins said, glancing in Kaleb's direction. "Now I will give you your first assignment, unless you have other ideas," Parkins said, looking in my direction.

I could tell he knew about my already-planned mission to rescue my family. I couldn't put anything else before that.

"Maybe we could do both at the same time. I can work it out," I assured him.

Parkins nodded his head and continued. "I believe you all know Noah's personal plans and missions already, but don't think his are any harder. The missions I will assign your newly formed team are no better, but no worse," Parkins explained.

He turned on the wall screen again, and this time a picture of a map appeared.

"The Rebal territory in Spain houses a very important asset to the Rebal organization. Tadmor," Parkins said darkly.

"Tad-what?" Ava asked.

"Tadmor. A supermax security prison built by the Rebal to house seriously valuable enemies," Parkins explained. "This map represents the strongest points, the weakest points, and the outline and building structure of the prison," Parkins pointed out.

Now the pieces fit together. The cells with meter-thick walls, no windows or bars, and a huge, huge wall. With three more walls behind it, and was that…an electric fence?

"It's going to be extremely hard getting in, but from our intelligence reports, it has something that you may want inside, Noah," Parkins said.

"What do you mean?" I asked.

"Your brother, Levi," Parkins replied.

The news hit me like a ton of bricks.

"What! Why is he there?" I nearly yelled, standing up from my chair.

"Please, please settle down," Parkins ushered. I sat back down, barely able to hold my anticipation.

"It seems your brother has the extremely rare power of the ability to see into the future, and possibly even more. Blade intends to use your brother to see the outcome of this war, but so far your brother hasn't said anything. They sent him to prison as punishment, although he is visited every day.

The news made me want to scream. My brother wasn't talking because for all I knew he couldn't. His whole life he'd lived in a mute world, seeing things ahead of time. I had to get him out of there.

"But, remember, I wouldn't send you on this mission if I didn't get something from it either. Our Tripartite leader for Mexico and South America is there, Dr. Ibal, our scientist from Peru. He has gained significant and perhaps war-changing information about the Rebal. With him we'll know possibly how and where the Rebal have staged and planned their attacks," Parkins explained. "With him, the war effort will increase dramatically."

Dr. Ibal and Levi. I had to rescue both. This was going to be harder than I thought.

"Remember, this isn't the hardest prison to break into, but it's far from the easiest. Listen to my plan and perhaps you will succeed," Parkins said slowly. "There will be two task forces. One for getting you in, and one for getting you out. Getting in will be easy. Getting out is the trickier part, at least getting out with everyone," Parkins warned.

We all turned our focus directly on him. It could be a matter of life or death.

"To get in, we'll need Jane, Kaleb, and Morri. Jane will be able to turn invisible, but because of her condition, things might be difficult. With her, you will be able to locate the cells each of our targets are stationed in. Jane will sneak in, find where their cells are, and come out and tell you. The difficulty of the mission could entirely depend on the areas they are being held. Once you figure out the areas, Kaleb's and Morri's jobs will start. Kaleb will climb up the electric fence and walls and, with Morri telling him how, disable the electricity and open the prison gates," Parkins explained.

"I will die. The electricity will kill me," Kaleb finally spoke up.

"We will give you gloves that are resistant to electricity," Parkins assured him.

Kaleb looked like he was going to say something, but Parkins cut him off.

"And boots."

Kaleb didn't reject.

"Once the walls are opened and the electric fence is disabled, there will most likely be guards by then. With the help of Ava, Zack, and Noah, you will take them out and put on their uniforms. It doesn't matter if they don't fit," Parkins said seriously.

"Won't we look suspicious?" Morri asked.

"The girls more so. But I believe the boys will be fine. Rebal rules enforce that no questioning of membership be allowed. Of course, that only applies for men because fights break out over it. If you girls are questioned, the boys will explain that you're giving a tour to Rebal inspectors," Parkins explained.

"Really?" I asked.

"Prisons are inspected every day. It will be normal for the guards," Parkins reassured me. "With Jane's guidance again, you will locate the cells, and with Morri bypass the locks," Parkins went on.

"I don't know much about hacking," Morri admitted.

"That doesn't matter. We have a surprise for you," Parkins smiled then winked at her.

Morri got red in the face, embarrassed and confused.

"Once you get them freed, Noah, Zack, and Ava will clear a path through the prison with their powers. The Rebal will be no match from an attack within the prison walls," Parkins said, almost delighted. "From there Jayce will get the portable wheeler we send with him out of his bag and make a getaway," Parkins finished.

"I'm fine with getaway driver. Used to it," Jayce joked. His normal self was already coming back.

Parkins smiled. "Good, we'll need all the experience we can get."

Parkins clapped his hands together, making a perfect ending.

"Your ship will be waiting at Washington, DC," he added.

"Isn't that where the government pretty much lives?" Zack asked.

"Of course it is. The president knows nothing of the Tripartite other than we are another regiment to his defense force. We carry out missions the government gives us but never tell them of the missions we commence. Then they'd be suspicious. Very suspicious," Parkins assured us.

"I can't wait to go. I want to rescue Levi now," I ordered.

"Wish granted, but until Kaleb agrees to assist you, there's no way you can accomplish your mission without him," Parkins said.

"We've figured things out. We'll probably be able to do it," Zack said.

"I don't doubt you one bit. But accomplishing your mission may require injury, maybe even death without Kaleb," Parkins explained.

He was right. We needed Kaleb.

"Don't worry. I'll sort him out," Zack said, popping his knuckles.

Kaleb didn't even flinch. Did he even hear him?

"There will be no violence! I will sort it out. I promise he will aid you. As you just saw, I have my way with words," Parkins said fast.

I hoped he was right.

CHAPTER 34

War Declared General Omen

General Omen, leader of the Belgium Rebal regiment, walked speedily to Dr. Blade's quarters. This was the biggest news he'd received in his whole life, and he was eager to be a part of the fight with the Rebal for once. As the general of one of the smallest Rebal forces, he tended to be uninvited or ignored in many cases, even as a general. This, he hoped, would change that.

He could barely control his anxiety as his hand touched the cold doorknob to Blade's quarters. It was now or never.

He turned the doorknob and quickly opened it, not waiting for permission.

Dr. Blade's eyebrows raised in surprise.

"What might you want, Omen?" Blade asked sharply.

"I promise you won't be disappointed," Omen assured him as he sat in the plush sofa in front of Blade.

"Finally. Something worth my time. Proceed," Blade said, almost happily.

"We have received contact, or information, if you will, on… the enemy," Omen chose his words carefully, trying to jeer Blade as much as he could.

Blade's happy expression turned confused.

"I'm sorry, the enemy?" he asked, perplexed.

"Yes, surviving witnesses of the attack told us everything, if not more than we'd hoped for," Omen declared.

"Go on," Blade said, leaning forward to catch every word.

"A German escapee from the Berlin complex, Kaleb, with climbing abilities, had a tracking and camera system in him when he escaped. Either he didn't know or forgot it was there," Omen continued.

"And you've been tracking him?" Blade said quickly.

"I hear a debate has been going through to declare war on the Tripartite or not, and clearly you have lost that debate," Omen added. "This is sure to gain you the upper hand."

Blade remembered the debate, and a sour frown formed across his face. He'd tried to order an attack on this new threat, or Tripartite, but many choice generals feared that the war against the world could not be won if powers died, but they didn't know he didn't know how powerful the Tripartite force was in the first place. He might be Blade, but even the mother bear has limits of power. But this news Omen had might be able to change all of that.

"We've tracked him through camera as far as the French coast, and who found him is quite interesting," Omen stated before turning out the lights.

Blade's holographic screen lit up, and a video started.

A boy, Kaleb probably, was running past buildings. Suddenly he turned around and saw four figures pursuing him. He took to a building and scaled its wall. A blast of energy forced him to fall off and land on the ground. A golden-haired boy appeared out of nowhere and secured his arms, then a stocky boy picked him up.

Blade knew these people anywhere. It was the four of the six escapees from Rebal International, Noah's freedom fighters. But this wasn't getting them anywhere. He looked at the video more intently and saw two fully equipped men with rifles and machine guns, and they all took the boy and led him to a boat. They had the Tripartite symbol. Sailors with the Tripartite symbol as well took the boy onto a ship, then the screen went black.

"We lost communication at that point. The boy's camera probably shut off or malfunctioned. But we haven't lost his tracking signal," Omen assured him.

"This is great. This is…revolutionary! Now all the Rebal will know that the Tripartite really exist and that they can fight us! It seems a war is about to begin…" Blade trailed off at the thought.

Omen pressed a button on the remote, and a map lit up on the screen.

"This is where we have tracked him. Right now he is in Washington, DC. The kids are probably with him. We'll be able to take out the Tripartite forces and the escaped powers in surprise. Their lives will be short-lived," Omen said while grinning.

"Very good job, General Omen. I plan to reward you for this precious information you've given the Rebal," Blade said with excitement.

Omen couldn't stop the smile from spreading across his face.

He was about to leave when a voice stopped him.

"And be at the debate at twelve. I plan to use your evidence and your part of the story," Blade confirmed.

"Of course," Omen replied.

CHAPTER 35

Fear Unleashed
Jayce Smith

Jayce stepped out of the car and saw the place he'd always dreamed of going to, Washington, DC. After everything he'd been through, talking with Dr. Parkins and revealing his secret that he was afraid, he felt surprisingly better, lighter, like he'd set down the elephant he was carrying for so long. He'd expected also to be surprised when he saw the center of the US government, but it looked as normal as ever, with trimmed trees and bushes along paved sidewalks, drinking fountains everywhere, picnics, and children playing with balls and frisbees.

The only thing that set the landscape apart was the huge buildings that had so much history behind them. The Capitol building, the Supreme Court, the Washington Monument, and the crown jewel of them all, the White House. Seeing just one of them made him giddy with excitement. He'd loved history class and had always wanted to visit these places.

He knew that he'd only be here for a while, though. They'd have to go on their suicide mission in a minute, and he definitely was not looking forward to that.

Morri stepped out of the car next, looping her arm through his. So much had changed since they had gotten out of the cells. He and Morri had been the oddballs of the group at first, but now he thought he could trust her more than anyone. He joked around with her because he was nervous around her, though he knew he would never tell her why.

He also knew Morri needed him. To protect her, or to be with her, he still didn't know, but he had the true feeling that they needed each other.

"Wow. I never thought I'd ever see these places!" Morri remarked, looking at the amazing surroundings.

"Tell me about it. The only monument I thought I'd be seeing was Blade's statue in our cell hallway," Jayce snickered.

"That would've been inhumane!" Morri laughed. Jayce loved the way she laughed.

Noah and the others were out of the van now. Their mission was about to start. An agent stepped out of the car last. He was wearing the same thing that Brock and his team had been wearing.

"So what do you want us to do?" Zack asked.

"We must wait for the last power, Jane, to arrive before you depart. You and the others can explore for that amount of time. I have been given orders to accompany you wherever you go," the agent explained.

"I don't need a babysitter," Ava retorted.

"I'll keep an extra close eye on you for that, girl," the agent sneered.

Ava shot him a glare.

"It's fine. I'll take care of her," Noah assured him.

"You I can trust," The agent smiled.

Ava gave a look of unbelief before Noah turned her around and led them away. We could hear every insult she shot at the agent before she was gone.

"The rest of you are free to go too," the agent said coolly.

"I'll stay and wait for Jane," Zack replied.

"Suit yourself, big guy," the agent answered.

"Come on," Morri said, tugging Jayce's arm.

"Where are we going?" Jayce asked.

"A field trip," she replied happily.

She led him to the steps of the Capitol building. He had been hoping she'd take him to the White House, but he didn't tell her.

"You know about the history behind the Capitol building?" Morri asked.

"A little, it was built in 1902." Jayce replied.

"Nineteen-oh-four," Morri corrected. And those were the finishing touches.

"It'd be nice to remember everything like you do," he said.

"It's actually kind've complicated remembering things," Morri replied. "It's like I have to scroll down a screen to find the right link to a memory. For me to be smart, I have to plan things out ahead of time. I planned out telling you about the Capitol when I got you to come with me," Morri added, her cheeks burning a bright red.

"I also know it was almost burnt down by the French in 1820," Jayce said.

"Eighteen fourteen, it was the British." Morri smiled.

Jayce reached over and laid his hand on her's. She shuddered at his touch but then relaxed.

"You know I was testing you, right?" Jayce laughed.

"What?" she yelled, then hit his arm.

Jayce laughed, and she fell on his shoulder then stayed there.

"I've been thinking," Morri said softly. "That when this is all over, we can go away, run, and live our own lives," she said, savoring the idea.

"Maybe we can. But with Blade, in a way, that will never happen," Jayce said sadly.

"Right," she said. "But after he's gone?"

Jayce thought about it. Leaving everyone behind, striking out on their own. What about the others? But the thought of him and Morri...together.

"I—"

Crkkkkk! The earth suddenly shook, knocking Jayce and Morri off the steps.

"Gah!" Morri gasped, holding her head in her hands.

Jayce scrambled to his feet and lifted her head up. "Are you okay?" he asked, worried.

"I'm fine. But what was that?" she said, wincing.

Jayce looked into the horizon.

Shkkkkk! The ground split beneath them, and they fell.

"Ahhhhhh!" Morri screamed. Jayce tried unsuccessfully to grab ahold of something to stop their fall to stop their descent.

Jayce looked at the ground below them then up again. The Capitol was gone. They were falling down a canyon that came out of nowhere. He had an idea right at that moment.

The second his feet hit the ground, Jayce went sonic.

His feet were going so fast that Jayce barely felt the impact. With Morri in his arms, he raced up the sloping canyon. Jayce saw that the sides were closing in and fast. A boulder snapped off a ledge and came rolling down the slope. He made a sharp turn, and the huge rock barely missed his back. Jayce had always run in open places, not narrow passes.

A cold sweat broke out. He lost faith. Jayce thought they would never make it out as the light faded and darkness took its place. Then he saw Morri's face, scared and frightened.

If Jayce wasn't running for him, then he would run for Morri. Jayce pumped his legs harder than ever, and the light returned.

He raced around broken ledges and jumped over ridges and slopes. Finally Jayce saw the grass of the park. He bolted upward and landed with a thud on the soft grass.

Morri rolled off him gasping for air.

"We made it," he choked.

"We made it…"

Fooom! The walls must have collided, and a huge shockwave rippled outward. He and Morri were flung into the air again, this time landing in the dirt.

"Jayce," Morri squeaked.

Jayce regained focus and stood up weakly.

He looked up and saw a shower of rocks heading toward them.

"Hurry!" he grunted, rolling Morri over. He'd lost the strength to pick her up and needed her to stand.

She rose wearily to her knees then collapsed in his arms. Jayce dragged her over to a nearby bench and rolled her under it, then he dropped his body over he's to shield her from the fear that had been unleashed on them.

When the avalanche of rocks ceased, he was surprised that he and Morri were still in one piece.

Morri tried to get up but grabbed her leg and winced.

"Where will we go now?" she asked, traumatized.

"We need to find the others. Now," Jayce replied.

CHAPTER 36

Power against Power
Noah Tone

I had felt the two tectonic plates collide before it even happened. The stress in the earth sent off vibrations that I could feel and track better than anyone on earth, by far.

I had been in midsentence talking with Ava when I sensed what would happen. I led her to a fountain, close to a car if we needed to get into it. Then it happened. It was so fast, but just far away enough that I only stumbled a bit, but then I almost fell. This time it was Ava that caught me. I wasn't embarrassed that she could've saved my life.

"Noah! Jayce and Morri are over there!" Ava said, panicked after the tremor.

I could only hope that Jayce raced them out in time.

"Let's go meet up with Zack. If Morri and Jayce got out in time, I'm sure that's where they'll go," I replied. We sprinted to where the agent dropped us off, and when got there, we saw a huge boulder cratered in the earth. This was a very powerful earthquake, but I hadn't expected it to fling rocks this far.

"Oh no. Zack..." Ava started.

Blam! The rocks splintered into a million pieces, and Zack stood up slowly, chucking a remaining part of the boulder off his back.

"He still lives!" I laughed.

"It'll take more than a rock to take me out," Zack grunted. "What happened?"

I took in the surroundings. In the distance where Jayce and Morri had been, in its place a huge canyon was formed.

"An earthquake in the middle of DC?" Ava asked, perplexed. People and witnesses swarmed the disaster zone, careful not to get too close.

Ava was right. This had to be the biggest coincidence ever to even be real. More likely it was on purpose. Before I could say anything, Jayce was running toward us, Morri limping along with him.

"Morri! Jayce!" Zack yelled.

I waved my hands to show them where we were.

Jayce finally met us, sweating and out of breath. Morri was clutching her leg. She was injured.

"Do you know how this happened?" Ava asked them.

"I have no idea. Morri and I were at the Capitol building when the earthquake knocked us down a canyon that came out of nowhere. I had to race her out as fast as I could run to even get us out alive," Jayce panted.

"This is crazy. Someone is behind this," Zack replied.

"I have a feeling we'll find out who soon enough," I added.

"Too soon?" a voice behind us snickered.

We all spun around and saw a tan boy with dark hair going down to his eyebrows.

"Ian," Zack growled. "What do you want?" he sneered.

"Zack, I'm honestly happy to see you here. I thought Blade got rid of you. I thought I'd never settle the score with you." Ian laughed.

"It was him," Zack told all of us. "He's a level three elemental power, one of Blade's favorites," Zack said with disgust.

"I'm surprised you remembered," Ian said coldly.

"He has some sort of earth power then, right?" Morri asked.

"You saw what I can do. Now come with me and I won't have to do it again," Ian ordered. "The last thing we need is a power versus power." He laughed.

"Where are you taking us, back to the dump we just escaped from? I don't think so," Jayce said loudly, stepping forward.

Ian rubbed his forehead.

"Please don't make this hard. I don't think either of us wants that," he said under his breath.

"We're not going back to Blade, and if we have to fight for it, we will!" I shouted.

"You had your chance," Ian said without emotion, and suddenly a rocky spire shot up from the ground, taking Ian up with it. He had to be at least a hundred feet in the air.

"Come down here, you coward!" Zack screamed, charging the pillar. He smashed into it with all his might, making it nearly toppled over.

I sensed another shockwave of earthquakes coming. They were going to happen all around us.

"Stay close!" I shouted and encased us in a protective shield of vibrations.

The earth shook and the ground rose above us then started falling inward on us.

The moment the earth hit my shield, I almost passed out. I could only hold this up for another minute at tops.

Ava realized and pulled the earth down around us with her gravity.

I let the shield down and breathed out heavily.

"Thanks," I said.

"Anytime," Ava replied.

People were flocking around the battle. Those who got to close got hit by rocks, and others were flung backward hundreds of feet. Eventually people just started to run around pointlessly. This was all Ian's doing. He was going to bring us down, and DC with it. We had to come up with a plan and quick.

"Okay, guys, were gonna have to split up if we want to take this guy down. He'll have to keep track of all of us at once. That'll put pressure on him!" I yelled over the noise.

I looked at Zack smashing down stone walls that Ian had created to protect his spire and smiled.

"Looks like one of us already has a plan." I laughed. "Okay, I'll do my best to contain his earthquakes with my vibrations. I know ahead of time when they'll strike," I explained. "Jayce, you try to run up to Ian and pin him down. Hope you have enough energy left. Ava, you help Zack in bringing Ian to the ground. Up there he's safe. Down here all of us will be able to attack him. Morri, if this plan fails, you'll be in charge of making a plan B. We're going to be counting on you, so stay out of danger." I ordered.

She nodded her head in agreement.

"If Jane comes, she'll run to Zack. He'll do everything to protect her. Is everyone ready?" I asked.

"Ready!" the team said in unison.

"Then let's show them what the First Strike can do!" I said proudly.

We all split off. The battle had begun.

CHAPTER 37

Fist to Stone
Zack Gupta

Zack relentlessly smashed into the earth and stone walls that stopped him from strangling Ian. Ian had been the one who informed Blade about him and Jane disobeying orders at Rebal International. He had betrayed them.

He wouldn't fight Blade, but he'd be happy to fight Ian.

"Urrgh," Zack grunted as his fist smashed through another wall. Like all the others, his power had limits, but he was too full of rage to stop pounding the earth and stone. With the help of others, he'd get to Ian. He'd do it.

Suddenly, a rain of boulders fell toward him. This was one of Ian's favorite tricks, and it worked well.

Zack put his hands up, preparing for impact.

A boulder smashed into him with so much force that his legs were ankle deep in the solid earth.

He hefted the boulder above his head and looked at the spire that Ian was perched on. He saw Jayce slowly gaining ground up the spire, but a boulder would always force him back down.

That's it! he thought. He waited for Jayce to get halfway up the slope, then waited for Ian to chuck a boulder toward Jayce, then threw the boulder he carried with all his might. The boulder spiraled faster than he'd intended it to go, and it smashed violently with

Ian's boulder, forcing it off track. Jayce continued up the slope and pounced on Ian, forcing him down.

"Strike one," Zack mumbled to himself, grinning happily.

CHAPTER 38

What Goes Up Must Come Down
Ava Jones

Ava could almost hear a cheer go up when Jayce reached the top of the pillar. She'd been busy pulling Ian's earth walls and rock spire into the ground, having no effect on them because they'd just build up again. Green flashes were coming from every side of the earth walls from Noah keeping earthquakes contained outside of the places where they were. At least others were having success.

Suddenly Jayce fell off the spire. He was about to hit an earth wall when he zoomed back up toward the spire again. That was a relief.

Ava suddenly realized she'd had the chance to pull down the walls when Jayce had Ian pinned down. She hadn't taken the chance.

She was suddenly angry with herself. She had to be focused on her part, not others.

She put her hands to the ground and slowly started to rise. She continued to rise until she was above the earth walls and still continued up. She could see everyone from here, Noah blasting back earthquakes, Zack deflecting boulders crushing on him and punching through the walls, Jayce speeding up the spiral, and Morri hiding by the White House steps, one of the few buildings that hadn't yet been destroyed. She raised higher still until she was level with Ian.

When he saw her, his expression was unfazed.

"Get down before I blast you to Chicago," he growled.

This was what Ava wanted, to keep him distracted.

"Stop before I turn you to paper," she shot back.

"You're Gravity Girl, aren't ya? Heard a lot about you. Saw the bodies of the guards you pancaked. Actually felt sorry for them," Ian said darkly, still focusing on the others below him.

A sudden wave of guilt and pain washed over her. She hated doing that to people. Hated hurting people at all.

No, Ava! He's messing with you! she scolded herself.

"I won't tell you again. Get down," Ian sneered, now looking her in the eye.

"No, you're the one going down," Ava said quietly.

She pulled gravity with all her might, and Ian's spire of rock snapped. She wasn't going to flatten him. He knew she wouldn't. Ava was going to teach him the laws of gravity.

Ian looked at her, eyes fiery and enraged.

"What are you doing?" he yelled, a hint of fear in his voice.

"Did you not know? What goes up must come down," Ava said simply.

Ian's expression turned terrified, and he tried to jump off his spire, but it was too late. It tumbled to the ground, taking him with it.

CHAPTER 39

Race Ended
Jayce Smith

Jayce was confused when he saw the spire toppling down. He'd been getting ready to race back up there and attempt to knock Ian off, but he'd already tried and knew Ian was stronger than him, even though he'd never admit it.

He raced out of the way of the falling spire as it collided with the ground, sending rocks flying every which way. He hid behind a large boulder to avoid raining rocks.

When the dust cleared, Ian was nowhere to be seen. They'd won?

The others gathered around the spire, happy and confused expressions on their faces. They were all happy it was over, but how had the spire fallen?

Ava suddenly floated down from the sky, landing on the soft grass without a sound.

"Should we wait for Jane now?" she asked.

"You did this?" Noah asked, happy as ever.

"Laws of gravity, really." She giggled.

Noah wrapped her in a hug. It was awkward for everyone for a while.

When they parted, Zack was the first to speak up. "If Jane was here, is she okay?" he asked.

They all gave each other uncertain looks.

"No," Zack said. "The van is still gone. She's not here yet," he said hopefully.

"You may be right, but—" Noah started.

Zack stormed off, clearly not wanting to hear what Noah had to say.

"If we won, then we should clear out of here," Jayce said. "We don't want some news lady interrogating us."

Everyone nodded their heads in agreement.

They were just passing the White House when the ground began to rumble.

"No way," Morri said. Terrified, she grabbed Jayce's arm for comfort.

Foom! The ground rumbled unsteadily. Suddenly the ground split between them and the White House stairs. Was it Ian's ghost?

Blam! The White House suddenly split in half. Chunks of white stone started flying toward them. Terror had set in. The race wasn't over.

CHAPTER 40

Downfall of the Greatest Noah Tone

I stood in horror as I took in the unreal scene. Ava gripped onto me tightly as the White House started to sink under the earth. My emotions were mixed with anger and fear as the greatest symbol of power of the greatest nation on earth fell. How could this be? Ava had killed Ian. We all saw it.

Without warning, the White House burst into millions of pieces, rock, earth, and metal flying at us in a hail of horror. I pulled Ava along with me, the others following my lead, and led her to a fallen building, smashing open a window so we could get in. A piece of rock cut my shoulder blade as we filed inside, and I grimaced in pain. A group of boulders came next, and I jumped into the window just in time to escape. I landed on Ava and put my body over hers to shield her from the rainfall of stone. When the rumbling stopped, I found that we were trapped by two boulders blocking the window. We couldn't get out any other way because stone and earth had caved us in the building. We were trapped. If I shot them away, I knew the boulder over us would fall down and kill us. We had to come up with a plan before we went out anyway. I rolled off Ava, and she intertwined her fingers with mine. The light was dim inside the building, only coming through cracks that the boulders had made.

I looked around and saw an arm sticking out of the debris and almost threw up.

Jayce and Morri found their way to us and settled down.

"Ian's still out there," Ava said, her voice jittery.

"What do we do now?" Jayce asked.

"I have a plan B," Morri offered.

"Will it work now?" I asked, annoyed.

"If we get out, it will," Morri replied.

"What is it then?" Ava asked.

"We all know that Ian has earth powers, so I was thinking if we took that power away from him, then he'd be powerless," Morri explained.

"This is nuts. Earth is everywhere," I replied.

"Washington, DC, isn't far from the coast. If we force him into the water, he'll be powerless," Morri added.

"Ian is going to stand his ground. He'll stay in one spot the whole fight, like he did the last time. I should know," Jayce put in.

Morri seemed stumped.

"What if we force him into the air?" Ava started. "I could lift him off wherever he is, and if he isn't touching the earth, he can't do anything," she explained.

"Why didn't you flatten him before?" I asked.

Ava looked away from me.

"You know I hate doing that, Noah," she whispered.

I started to grow angry. "We could've gotten rid of him, but you were too scared!" I yelled.

"I have my reasons!" Ava shot back.

"If you had killed just one person, one, then all these other people wouldn't be dead," I said softer this time.

Ava looked at the bloody arm and started to cry.

She fell against me and shuddered.

"It's okay," I said. "Maybe he is gone and this is just an aftershock," I said hopefully.

"I highly doubt that. Hitting the White House would be Ian's main target, plus we were next to it," Morri said bitterly.

I knew she was right.

Ava wiped a tear from her face and looked up at me.

"I'm sorry," she whimpered.

"It's okay. I saw him talking to you up there. He was probably messing with you," I said soothingly.

"If Ava's plan works, then what battle would we have won anyway? I bet half the city is dead now," Jayce said.

Another rumble shook the building, and a boulder crashed not too far from us.

"Wait, something's wrong," I said, panicked.

"What is it?" Morri asked.

"Where's Zack?"

Chapter 41

Strike Two, Strike Three, Out
Zack Gupta

Zack walked along the wreckage of DC. The landscape was just like the pictures they saw with Parkins of the destroyed cities. It was the "natural" apocalypse all over again.

It had all happened so fast, the White House now destroyed, the raining earth and stone. He'd been hit at least fifteen times. His shirt was torn, and his pants were ripped. His power was almost out. If Ian was out there, he'd stand little chance against him.

He fell to his knees, tired and dehydrated. Jane could be dead, but he couldn't force himself to believe it.

He looked at his arm, a deep gash across it. He was losing blood fast. He never bled, not unless his strength was going out.

"Well, if it isn't the mighty Zack." A wicked voice laughed.

Zack turned his head around slowly. It was Ian, and he didn't look much better than he did, but he was hiding his pain. His face was covered in dirt, and blood was staining through his pants. His shirt was gone, revealing perfect abs and a strong chest.

"How could you have done this?" Zack growled.

To his surprise, Ian sat down next to him.

"Believe me, I didn't want it to come to this," Ian said, unconvincingly.

Zack stared at the landscape, frames of once-tall, brilliant buildings, a once-lush, grass-filled environment, now a desert of earth and rock, buildings on fire, and others halfway buried in the ground. Jane might be dead because of him.

"Blade gave me orders, and I followed them," Ian breathed out heavily.

"So what, he'd give you a part of DC to own? Nice deal now that it's a junkyard." Zack laughed menacingly.

"No, so we could cleanse the world, make a world of just us, just powers. Why does the idea not appeal to you? You and Jane could be happy, free," Ian said with reasoning.

"She might be dead," Zack growled.

Ian took a step back, realizing his mistake, then smiled.

"She's not dead. I saw her and the others are trapped in a building," he said.

"Why didn't you kill them?" Zack asked.

"I was looking for you, Zack," he explained.

"Why?" he asked again.

"Because you can be with me. With Blade, with the Rebal! If you join us, we will take over the world! And you will be given a part of it!" Ian said happily.

How could Zack know that Ian was telling the truth about Jane, about him getting part of the world? He knew what he had to do.

Ian offered his hand. "Well?" he asked.

Zack slowly stood and extended his hand toward Ian's. He grabbed it and was about to shake when Zack squeezed with all his might.

"Ahhh!" Ian yelled, struggling against Zack's grip. He flung Ian twenty feet forward, and he landed on a rock with a crack.

Ian started coughing up blood, and Zack slowly walked toward him. When Zack looked over Ian, his eyes were filled with madness.

"You may have beaten me, but you will never stop Blade. You will never stop the plague of powers," he said groggily.

Zack grabbed his neck and squeezed. Ian's eyes rolled back. He was dead.

Zack was overcome with emotion. Relief, sadness, anger.

He knew Ian had to go. Blade had complete control over him. There was no reasoning with Ian.

Zack looked away from Ian's dead body and started to search for the others.

Chapter 42

Only the Beginning
Noah Tone

Morri, Jayce, Ava, and I shifted uncomfortably in the enclosed building. The only way we could get out was to receive help from outside.

There had been no more shockwaves or tremors for a while now. Either Ian went to set an earthquake somewhere else or he'd died somehow or at least gotten injured. I could only hope it was the last two.

Ava laid her head on my shoulder in the darkness.

"Wer'e going to die here, aren't we?" she asked, looking at Jayce and Morri huddled in the far corner of the room where there was light.

The dust and stench were making it hard to breathe.

Ava started sobbing into my shirt, and I was running my hand through her hair slowly.

We stayed like that for a while then heard footsteps outside.

"Ian!" Jayce hissed.

"We can't let him hear us!" Morri whispered.

I looked through a crack in the rocks and saw a familiar face. It was square-shaped, and he had stocky shoulders, but he looked tired and weary. It was Zack!

"Guys, it's Zack!" I yelled.

Everyone swarmed to my corner, looking through the cracks in the rocks.

"Zack! Zack! Over here!" we all yelled.

He stopped and walked toward the sound, stopping at the blocked-off window.

"Zack! We're trapped! Lift the rocks away!" Morri shouted.

Zack hefted one rock away, quickly throwing more to the side until a gaping hole appeared. Ava went out first, I was next, then Jayce and Morri.

"Ahhhh! This feels so much better! Morri said, breathing in the air.

I was shocked. The landscape looked like one from a ghost town. Everything was replaced with rocks and earth. It was the saddest thing I'd seen in my whole life.

"No, this is terrible," Ava whispered.

"I was wrong. Maybe a handful of survivors are still out there," Jayce said in shock.

Morri turned pale.

Zack waited next to the hole, like someone else would come out.

"Where's Jane?" he asked.

"Jane? You've seen her?" Ava asked.

"Crud. He was lying," Zack said in defeat.

"Who was lying?" I asked.

"Ian," Zack said heavily.

"Ian? You saw him?" I asked.

Jayce and Morri ran in. "What?" they both said.

"Did you get hurt? Is he still out there?" Jayce asked.

We waited for an answer.

"I killed him," Zack said darkly.

"Whoa," Ava breathed out.

"How?" I asked.

"Tried to reason with me. Didn't turn out well," Zack replied.

"Big, big change of story," Jayce explained.

"We need to find Jane now," Zack said, like it was obvious.

I wanted to ask more questions, but I knew Zack didn't want to answer them.

Three figures started running toward us. More powers? Ian back from the dead again?

We got prepared, already prepared for battle, when a voice shouted out.

"Zack! Zack!" someone cried.

"Jane? Jane!" Zack shouted. He charged toward the figure and collided with her, wrapping her in a hug. "I thought you were dead!" Zack said, tears flowing down his face.

"What happened? I felt an earthquake, and the agent had to drive away from DC. He said that he needed to get me and Kaleb out of danger," she cried.

"Kaleb? He agreed to come?" I asked. Kaleb stepped up behind them, the same somber expression he always wore.

"I wouldn't push it," Ava whispered in my ear. I nodded in agreement.

The agent stepped ahead of Jane and Zack and said, "The docks are gone, but a ship from NYC is coming to take you instead. Don't think you won anything. The battle is far from over," the agent warned.

"I've gotten used to people saying that," Jayce said unhappily.

"Keep in mind, this is only the beginning," the agent added.

When we were all grouped together, I knew the journey that lay ahead of us would be hard, but if it meant saving my brother, I'd take it.

"Come on, First Strike, we have a mission to complete."

End of Book One

About the Author

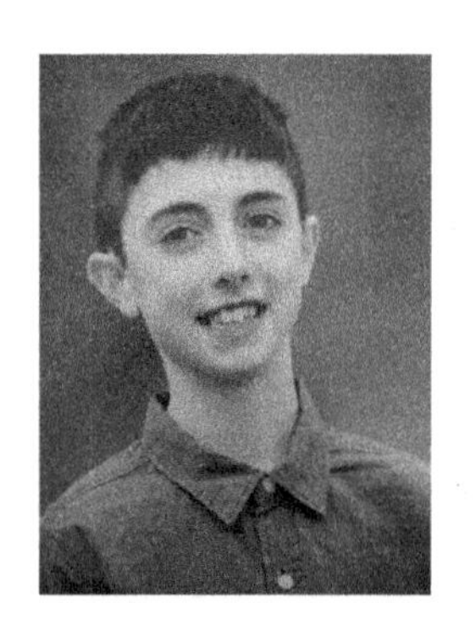

Noah Cotter lives in Platte City, Missouri, with his two parents, four brothers, and one sister. He began working on his novel when he was twelve, and when he is not around his huge family, trying to set a good example to his five younger siblings, or wishing summer break would never end, the thirteen-year-old spends his spare time outside, playing sports, reading, drawing, or whatever he feels like doing. He loves dinosaurs, and besides being an author, he dreams of becoming a paleontologist.

CPSIA information can be obtained
at www.ICGtesting.com
Printed in the USA
FSHW010643160420
69217FS